Hormones, Hexes, & Exes

Menopause, Magick, & Mystery

JC BLAKE

Published by Redbegga Publishing, 2020.

This is a work of fiction. Similarities to real people, places, or events are entirely coincidental.

HORMONES, HEXES, & EXES

First edition. July 7, 2020.

Written by JC BLAKE.

To all women.

May you grow in power as you age and hold magic in your hearts.

Chapter One

Crazy as it sounds, it was a bat that tipped me off!
It began to swoop above my head as I tottered across
the lawn to fetch another bottle of Prosecco—the bottle my
husband, Pascal, had promised to bring back from the wine
chiller ten minutes ago. I'm not sure if it was the glass of champagne I'd downed as my fiftieth birthday was being toasted, or
the numerous freshly mixed cocktails Aunt Loveday had pre-
sented me with, or perhaps the fumes from the 'cigarettes' some
of my more 'adventurous' guests were smoking, that skewed my
thinking, but the bat seemed to be on a mission to attack me!
After a second and lower swoop, I veered away from the house
and across the lawn, cursing the high-heels Vanity had tricked
me into wearing—such a dumb choice for a garden party! On
the third swoop, I began to panic and headed for the closest
safe-haven, a flower-covered archway. On the fourth, convinced that the flapping beast would get tangled in my hair as it
came at me from the darkness like a tiny, leather-winged Exocet
missile, I ran through the archway and into my 'secret' garden.

Until that moment, the evening had been perfect.

Forty-six birthday party guests, mostly family but with a
good number of friends, close neighbours, and my husband's
work colleagues and their partners, filled our garden. The air
was heavy with the scent of honeysuckle and lavender, the

1

chiminea was throwing out a warming glow, and strings of fairy lights sparkled against the backdrop of dark hedges and spiralled around trees. Glasses chinked, guests laughed and chattered and, to top it all, an enormous silver moon hung like a magical orb in the midnight blue sky. I had also managed to lose eight of the twenty-six pounds of extra weight that I constantly battled with, and my confidence had taken a boost—life was good!

The heady aroma of chocolate-scented clematis that engulfed the archway filled my senses, but it was the giggling laughter of a woman, and stifled murmurs of a man, that caught my attention. The bat swooped for a final time, chirruped, then disappeared into the night sky. Already more than tipsy, with a tingling sensation beginning to itch at my fingertips, I steadied myself and stepped into the 'secret' garden, curious to discover which of my guests had sloped off. Looking back, I think my subconscious already knew the truth, it was just doing a great job of protecting me. The bat had a different opinion!

Those next moments changed my life, and me, forever.

It's difficult to explain the way that discovering the man you consider your closest friend, the one you have trusted with the most intimate, vulnerable part of yourself, the man you chose as your mate for life, is betraying you and the love you built your shared world around. Floored, devastated, and gutted, just do not cut it. In that moment, my soul was scraped from my body, pushed through a grinder, and crumbled into a thousand tiny pieces.

I was broken.

I sobered instantly.

I had to look twice to make sure I wasn't imagining it, but there it was, my husband's hand on another woman's bottom. Selma Maybrook was our much younger, effortlessly glamorous, neighbour, a woman who oozed a sensual charm that even I was aware of. With her well-toned curves unpadded by unwanted fat, glossy dark curls without sign of grey, and breasts that hadn't yet sagged, she was a magnet for male attention. It didn't seem to matter that her wealth was the product of three lucrative divorces, men still buzzed around her like flies to a dung heap. Only last month, over a glass of wine at our kitchen table, Selma had confided to us that she was lonely, that her bed seemed huge and empty, and that she was perhaps ready to find Mr. Right—again. It hadn't crossed my mind that her targets were set on my Mr. Right! When Pascal gave her pert and amply rounded bottom cheek a lascivious squeeze then leant in to nuzzle her neck, I knew my marriage was over.

There were only twenty steps between me and the canoodling pair, but even though every ounce of my flesh wanted to run across that space, wrench the two apart, and vomit my pain all over them, I stood frozen, and watched. Some part of me wouldn't accept what it was seeing, a tiny, pathetic voice was telling me that I needed more evidence, that squeezing another woman's bottom didn't mean that my husband was having an affair, that he'd had a lot to drink and wasn't really in control of himself, and that it was Selma who was leading him astray. With her pert breasts, slim waist, curvaceous hips, and come-to-bed eyes, she was the guilty party.

And then he began to kiss her—in earnest.

Seconds passed and it was obvious what was going to happen. Hands slipped over curves, mouths began to devour, then fingers began to unzip and unbutton. Somewhere above, the bat chirruped - *do bats even do that?* – and I went into attack mode. Well, my lame version of it.

"Hey!" I called as I took several steps towards the pair. To my complete surprise, they just ignored me and carried on molesting one another. "Hey!" I called again, a little louder—pip-squeak level. The bat chirruped again. "Alright!" I hissed at the winged irritant. "Hey!" I shouted, this time so loudly that my voice cracked under the strain. Selma stared right at me then, pressed up against the outhouse wall, her legs wrapped around my husband's hips. Pascal swung round, dropping Selma like a stone. He stood there, gormless, belt unbuckled, jeans slipping down his thighs, shirt tails barely covering his excitement as she scrabbled on the ground.

"Liv!" he gasped, stumbling over Selma as he hurriedly pulled at his jeans and tugged at the zipper. "It's not what-"

"Don't even try to say that it's not what I think it is. Even I can see that you were about to ..." I choked. I couldn't say it. "About to ..."

"Make love, Liv," Selma chimed in. She stood beside my husband with a proprietorial arm slipped through his.

"Make love!" I choked again, the pain pounding at my chest growing worse. "Love, Pascal?"

"Yes, that's right, Liv," Selma crowed. "We're in love!" As she said this her hand tightened around his bicep. "Tell her, Pascal!"

"Well ..."

What! He was actually going to agree with this maneater? A lightness began to fill - or is that empty? - my head.

Without waiting for Pascal to speak, Selma continued. "We're in love, and he's going to ask you for a divorce, Liv." She said this with such confidence that her words felt like a punch.

"A divorce?" I gasped for the word as my lungs refused to take in air. "Pascal?" Still mute, he made no effort to refute her words, and just stared back at me like a rabbit caught in head-lights, a very guilty rabbit that was about to be mown down.

"You neglect him, Liv. And a man like Pascal," she stroked a hand across his chest as she continued to grip his arm, "has his needs. You've had your chance, it's my turn now."

My anger began to rise. I had been giving Pascal what he needed for the last twenty-six years. I had even given up my own career to support his and give him what he needed! Sure, the 'romantic' side of things had slipped a little recently; most of the time I just wanted to get into bed and light up my kindle, but hell! I was fifty years old, overweight, and headed on a fast-speed train through the menopause. And marriage was about so much more than sex. "He's *my* husband, Selma! *My* hus-band. You have no right ..." My words faltered as my body let me down and began spiralling into one of its menopausal melt-downs. *Typical!* My face began to redden, and a hot tingling sensation uncurled from the centre of my body, radiating from my chest, across my shoulders, down my belly and through my limbs. My head buzzed and I felt giddy. I'd had hot flushes be-fore, but this one was off the scale. Sparks seemed to go off in my ears, and the heat coursing through my body was intense, particularly in my fingers. The tips fizzed. I had heard that hot flushes could be overwhelming, but this was ridiculous; I was on the verge of spontaneous human combustion!

Selma took my silence as weakness and began to document my lack of effort to 'satisfy' my neglected husband, knowledge that could only have come from Pascal himself. As she talked at me, building her case for spousal neglect, I did something that I had never done before – I totally lost it!

"Just shut up!" I screamed. "Shut up, shut up, shut up! You're a scheming, conniving, heinous slut!" To my complete surprise, Selma's flow of words stopped immediately. Her mouth moved, but no sound came out. For a moment she continued mouthing words like a fish gulping at water then, realising that her voice had vanished, grasped her throat. She tried again, but this time her jaw locked. Mouth wide open, and staring at me in terrified silence, her tongue flopped about like a fat, pink worm.

Overhead, the bat's chirrup sounded oddly like a giggle.

Chapter Two

I filled my glass with the last of the Prosecco as Aunt Loveday ushered the last guest from the garden. "Curse them both!" I said with ugly bitterness remembering the gloating smile on Selma Maybrook's face as, voice restored, she led my husband out of our house. From my seat in the garden I could see her house next door. I took another gulp of wine as her figure appeared at the bedroom window and she closed the curtains with a determined, and to me, joyful swish. My heart broke again knowing that my husband was in that room with her, about to climb into her bed and not ours. A painful sob built in my chest. "I wish they were dead!" I spluttered into my wine glass.

A collective hiss of disapproval immediately filled the air and a short rhyming couplet muttered by Aunt Thomasin was quickly repeated by Beatrix and Euphemia, the other aunts who had stayed to comfort me. Wallowing too deeply in my own grief, I took little notice of their mumbled words until Aunt Loveday returned.

"Well," she said with a clap of her hands and a happy lilt in her voice, "that's the last of the guests." The atmosphere around the table quickly brought her down. "What? What's wrong?"

"Oh, you mean other than that my husband has left me ... and on my fiftieth birthday!" I wailed, consumed by self-pity.

"She just cursed them, Loveday," Aunt Beatrix explained.

"And wished them death!" Aunt Thomasin finished in hushed and sombre tones. To add to her dramatic response, she glanced around the moonlit garden as though expecting something to come jumping out of the bushes.

Aunt Loveday sucked in her breath and muttered the same rhyme. I took note then. All four women were exchanging concerned glances.

"What? I didn't mean it ... well, I did, but not the death bit, not really."

"You must be careful, Liv," Aunt Loveday replied, scouting the dark beyond the prettily lit area of garden where my birthday party had come to such a spectacularly bad end, "with the choice of your words."

"We counteracted it as soon as she said it, Loveday," Aunt Euphemia added. Her voice too was overly, and uncharacteristically, sombre.

I chugged another mouthful of Prosecco, irked by their disapproval. "For goodness sake! It's just a saying. Anyone would think I was plotting their murder the way you four are going on." Ordinarily I would never be so disrespectful to my aunts, even at fifty years old, I still held them in the same awe I had as a child.

Since my parents' death in a car accident when I was only eighteen months old, the four sisters, Aunts Thomasin, Loveday, Euphemia, and Beatrix had collectively cared for me. Until my marriage, we had all lived together in the ancestral home, a sprawling fifteenth-century stone cottage sat in large grounds and surrounded by ancient woodland. Like so many things in our family, ownership went back numerous generations. We could trace our ancestry all the way back to the eleventh century - although the aunts often hinted at even older events and family members - but that knowledge was something I'd never taken an interest in despite numerous early efforts by the aunts to educate me.

Unable to hold back the tears, I sobbed into my glass as I swallowed the last mouthful of wine.

"She is in a state," murmured Aunt Thomasin.

"It's to be expected," Euphemia followed. "She has been in such ignorance for so many years."

"Denial really, darlings," Loveday added.

All four murmured "Hmm," simultaneously, each agreeing with the other.

Despite my alcohol-befuddled state their mutterings penetrated my self-pity and I was suddenly suspicious, defensively so. "Ignorant of what?" I presumed the 'ignorance' related to my inability to please my husband, "And what exactly am I in denial of? I've been a good wife!"

"Too good!" Thomasin said with vehemence.

"Too good for that philandering toad!"

"Adulterous cheating deceiver!"

"False-hearted recreant."

"That's my husband you're talking about ..." My words trailed off in another pathetic, self-pitying bout of weeping.

"It's time she knew."

All four nodded in agreement.

"Loveday, you're the ... eldest. I believe it's your place to explain."

"Thank you, Thomasin, for that reminder, but not by many years, and I don't think that I look a day older than yourself."

"Ladies! Now is not the time for debating who is ageing best!"

"Quite."

"Go on! Tell her then."

By now they had my full, albeit alcohol-fuelled, attention.

"Darling," Aunt Loveday began, "you may have noticed that we're," she gestured to the women gathered round, "a little different ..."

I nodded. My four aunts had always seemed so much more alive and vibrant than other women of their age. As all four hovered above me, each looking on with varying degrees of pity, and what I now realise was a mixture of elation and fearful anticipation, I began to see them with fresh eyes. In a strange trick of the moonlight, a sparkling haze of golden and silvery particles hovered around them seeming to ebb and flow. There really was something different about my aunts.

Aunt Loveday claimed to be the eldest, but in appearance there really was little difference between them. Each had their unique style, and although heading for the last portion of their years on this earth, none had the frailness of body, or mind, that so many elderly people had. As time passed, I had noticed how the irises of older people became faded, how their skin paled and slackened. Their hair, and lips, would thin and their muscles waste. None of this geriatric certainty had befallen my aunts. Despite claiming to be over seventy years old, if I were to stand beside them you would be hard pressed to tell the difference between us. In fact, they looked in better shape than me.

Aunt Loveday's slenderness was accentuated by the black outfits she generally wore. Although obvious she was an older woman, her skin was still smooth over high cheekbones and her jawline showed little sign of sagging. Vibrant green eyes were outlined by dark lashes, but it was her hair, a bright silvery-white, still thick and falling in full and luxurious curls that stole the show. Her simple outfits were accentuated by oversized and distinctive necklaces, brooches, and bracelets. Each golden piece was unusual, obviously artisanal, and decorated with interlinked dragons and other unfathomable creatures. I had never seen her in anything remotely 'modern'.

Raven-haired Aunt Thomasin had the least grey, but the wide streak of pure white that shot like a bolt of lightning through it was spectacular. The tallest of the four, she was also slender, with long fingers and nails always immaculately painted. She reminded me of the headmistress from the film, 'Miss Peregrine's Home for Peculiar Children', and seemed quite taken with the comparison, although was rather sniffy about the woman's powers. With her nipped waist, I suspected that she wore a corset beneath the Chanel-style suits she favoured.

Aunt Beatrix was the smallest, a tiny bird-like woman no taller than five feet with hair a cloud of the richest auburn with flashes of white at the temples. Often in full length skirts with shirts ruffled at the neck and sleeves, an apron covering her dress when at home, she reminded me of a petite, albeit kind, Victorian school mistress. On those occasions she ventured away from the cottage, she 'modernized' and wore a twin-set and pearls, very much in the style of Miss Marple. Of them all, I would call her the most 'spiritual' and she was often in the kitchen making salves and tinctures from herbs grown in their garden.

Unlike my other aunts, Euphemia kept her silver-white hair cropped short and favoured fitted jeans and casual shirt, often of the brightest white and always immaculate. She had a variety of shirts, some fitted, some larger without collars, and a number that reminded me of the undershirts worn beneath Elizabethan tunics with their embroidered and frilled, cuffs and collars. Large belts accentuated her small waist. How she wore heels at her age, day in day out, when my feet already hurt far too much to wear them for anything other than the most infrequent occasions, was a marvel to me.

Overweight, often flustered, and irritable, I was ridiculous in comparison to these elegant women who exuded a quiet power. My hair, once a rich strawberry blonde had darkened to mouse and although it was flashed with white at the temples, and had a sprinkling of light grey through the crown, there just wasn't enough of it to make the kind of impact my aunts managed so effortlessly.

All four wore the same wide silver bangle, hand forged and imprinted with various designs and inscriptions.

"Well," Aunt Loveday continued as the others waited with bated breath, "and I don't want to startle you, but we're different because we are witches ... and so are you."

Four pairs of eyes watched me with anticipation. Above our heads, the bat swooped and chittered.

Chapter Three

"Witches!" A derisory snort of disbelief was quickly replaced by uncertainty and a sensation of nausea swirling in my belly. I really should not drink on an empty stomach!

Aunt Thomasin handed me a cup of coffee, so strong that the rich aroma prickled at my nose. It was also laced with sugar, but I sipped it politely.

"That'll put hairs on your chest!" she smiled.

"That's something she doesn't need, Thomasin!" Aunt Loveday reprimanded.

I snorted the coffee then, laughing despite the horror of the past hour.

"She has enough to worry about with the hairs that are sprouting from her chin."

I began to squirm with mortification, my hand involuntarily reaching for my jaw, searching for the offending hairs.

"It's only a saying, Loveday. I didn't mean that it would actually *put* hairs on her chest!"

Beatrice giggled. "Do you remember Alice Swinson?"

Thomasin threw her a laughing glance. "Oh my! Yes, I do. The news on the grapevine was that it took her months of waxing and plucking to rid herself of the hairs."

"Well you did rather overdo it, Thomasin. How did that spell go ... Ah, yes, something about 'you will wake with a hairy chest.'"

"I think the phrase she used was, 'growing thatch across your breast.'"

Beatrice snorted with delight, her tiny frame heaving with laughter, a definite cackle.

"Now, now sisters, let's not scare the girl," Aunt Loveday interjected. "We're here to help Livitha, not cackle about past foes conquered."

"Well, then, I would say that it's the hairs on her upper lip that need the soonest attention," quipped Aunt Euphemia.

Four pairs of eyes scrutinised my face. My cheeks burned as the four women, none of whom showed signs of unwanted facial hair, discussed my appearance.

"Well, the sooner she's initiated the better," Aunt Loveday said with finality. Beatrix, and Euphemia nodded in agreement.

"You'll feel so much better once you've gone through the initiation." Aunt Thomasin laid a gentle hand over mine. "It's a very special ceremony." She stroked the bracelet on her wrist and smiled. "We have so much to tell you, Liv."

"She has so much to learn!" corrected Euphemia.

All four murmured in agreement, their gaze intent on me. Aunt Thomasin still seemed to be paying particular attention to my chin. I winced and lifted the coffee cup to hide my face.

"We should have put the 'hairy chest spell' on that denizen." Thomasin gestured to Selma's house, her tone was hopeful, almost a question.

"We've cast enough spells tonight, Thomasin. We've shown Livitha her husband's true desires."

Aunt Loveday's words, always chosen so carefully, immediately pricked at my suspicion. "How have you shown me Pascal's 'true desires'?"

"Well, you saw what he was ... doing ..."

"The dirty rascal!"

"Immoral adulterer!"

"Philandering rake!"

"Okay, okay!" I said as the list continued. "I get it. Pascal has cheated on me, but you said you had shown me his true desires. Explain!"

"Well, it was something that we had to do. You are on the cusp of an extraordinary time in your life, and we couldn't let you go forward with *that* man."

Confusion swirled. Did they have something to do with Pascal's deception? Had they set him up? Was Selma a honeytrap he had fallen into?

"You have completed your fiftieth year in this incarnation," Aunt Loveday gestured with a graceful sweep of her hand in my direction. "For us, the fiftieth year is one of discovery and growing power. We couldn't have Pascal, a man far beneath your status, holding you back."

"Far beneath my status? Holding me back? He's been my husband for twenty-six years and I love him ... What have you done?"

"We had to break the ties. You must join the coven without entanglements, darling."

"So ... let me get this straight. You've broken up my marriage so that I can join a coven!" I was flabbergasted. How could they be so cruel?

"No, Liv, it's not quite like that."

"Then explain exactly what it is 'like'," I countered, anger growing through my self-pity.

"He wasn't right for you, darling. He's had lots of affairs you know."

"What? No, that's not true!"

"It is I'm afraid, Livitha," Aunt Loveday explained. "And all I did was to cast a spell that revealed his true desires."

"So ... you forced him to ... cheat with that woman?"

"No, no darling-."

"We all know that he has been unfaithful."

The four women nodded. I think my eyes were blurred, but a shimmering haze of minute golden particles seemed to envelope them. I put it down to my tear-blurred vision and the dragonfly-shaped solar lights I'd so happily strung around the garden earlier in the day.

Thomasin continued. "Oh, yes indeed, the dirty rat."

"Pretty much since the beginning," Loveday added. She ran a finger through immaculate grey hair that perfectly framed her face with a gentle curl.

"Now that's not fair, Loveday," Euphemia countered. "It was at least ten years into the marriage before he started looking for fresh meat."

"What?"

"Oh, yes, that secretary of his," Aunt Loveday replied. "I'd quite forgotten about her!"

"How could you forget!" Beatrix interjected. "That little blonde with rather large ..." She made a gesture of a ballooning chest, her eyes growing larger for emphasis. I knew exactly who she referred to, Kayleigh Bright, a voluptuously attractive younger woman who had started work at Pascal's office at least sixteen years ago. A memory of jealousy and suspicion also pricked at me. Could it be true? If it was, he had looked for younger women even then, and our marriage was a sham!

"Yes, but don't worry dear, we saw that one off when it looked as though it was becoming serious."

My head thumped. "What? Serious?" My mind was fuddled, unable to process whether I should be more concerned about Pascal cheating on me for most of our marriage, or that this coven of cackling witches knew about it all along, and even 'managed' his infidelities.

"Does he know that you know about his ... other women." The pain was so bad as I said 'other women' that I had to take a moment to catch my breath. My whole world was falling apart. Everything I had thought was true was just a sham. "Did you confront him about her?"

"Oh, no! What happens in the coven stays in the coven," Beatrix said with a conspiratorial smile and Aunt Thomasin tapped the side of her nose with a knowing lift of her brows. My heart felt as though it were being ripped out, otherwise I would have laughed at the absurdity of it all.

"We just created a diversion for the girl."

"A very muscular Russian by the name of Sergei, if I remember rightly."

"Indeed it was, Thomasin."

"She became besotted ... with a little help."

"That was one of Euphemia's finer love potions, I have to admit," Loveday said.

"It's still working now," Euphemia beamed. "She writes to me every now and again. She's on her fifth child and very happy now they've moved into the countryside away from Moscow."

"Ahh, I do love a happy ending," beamed Beatrix. "It gives one hope. Now," she said with a glitter in her eyes, "back to Livitha's mess!"

I groaned and took another sip of sweet coffee.

Chapter Four

When I finally managed to get to bed, I fell asleep to the most lurid and bizarre dreams I had ever experienced where dark shadows danced around a fire and I swooped above the scene. Most of the dreams were laced with danger and mystery, fire and incantations, and a sense of ancient beings. Goblins, ghouls, witches, vampires, werewolves, dark fae and devils, only partially seen, inhabited the shadows. Selma Maybrook featured, as did Pascal, and others I didn't recognise. At one point a woman burned at a stake and I was filled with an insufferable grief. The colours were rich and vibrant. The voices crystal clear but often sing-song and indecipherable. I dreamt as though I had stepped into a film. I dreamt as though remembering past lives and events, as though my current life were a fragile shell within which it hid.

The next morning, I woke slowly, bathed in sweat, dipping in and out of that sleep-like state where dreams entwine with memories and what is real becomes blurred. For several minutes I struggled to separate the dreams from reality, but finally managed to keep my eyes open. Late morning sunlight bathed my room, the bedside clock showed that it was ten o'clock. Guilt washed over me. An early riser, I was always the first to be up and make Pascal a cup of tea and, in the past year, I had tak-

Chapter Five

The next few days were strange. The house was quiet without Pascal, and although he was usually absent for most of the day, and in recent years a good number of evenings during the week as well – how had I missed that enormous clue? – I missed having that one person to talk to, make a cup of tea for, or share a meal with. Just knowing that he was in the house was often enough to quell my loneliness. In the past, the distinctive roar of his car's engine would signal his homecoming, but now it signalled his betrayal. On the first two evenings I had moved to the window, watching with a heavy and pounding heart, nausea swirling in my belly, as his car rolled past our drive and turned into Selma's. After the second night, and after some less than sympathetic jibes from Lucifer, I promised to stop taunting myself by watching. I couldn't close my ears off though and had taken to turning up the radio during the times he would leave or return to his new 'home'.

Now Lucifer had revealed himself as my familiar, he had become more of a companion, but he was far more curmudgeonly than Pascal had ever been, and more demanding! I was still unsure whether I liked this 'new and improved' Lucifer and struggled to believe that he was only thirty-two years old. Somehow, he seemed far older, ancient almost.

On the fourth evening, sun flooded my kitchen with its mellow light as I washed the pots, placing a solitary bowl beside the spoon I had used to eat my soup. Both items sat beside a single mug. My bread roll remained untouched and I replaced it in the bread bin. Normally I would eat two soft and doughy rolls spread with plenty of butter, but my appetite had disappeared along with my husband. Supper had been a quiet affair and even Lucifer hadn't graced the table with his presence.

As I stared out of the kitchen window to my garden, Mr. Grayson held loppers to a branch that overhung his property. The lopping was a pretence, he barely snipped the leaves. "Nosey old sod!" I muttered, not caring if my voice carried through the open window, then nearly jumped out of my skin as the doorbell chimed and Pascal's voice rang out in the hallway.

"Liv!" His initial call was hesitant, but as he stepped into the hallway it became stronger.

He's back!

The noise of heels clacking across hallway tiles destroyed my hope, making my heart sink, each tap like a stab to the heart. She, the evil husband-stealing, man-eating denizen, was with him! I took a deep breath, heat rising on my cheeks. "Coming!" I called, determined not to allow my emotions get the better of me, and Aunt Loveday's advice repeating in my mind.

We met at the kitchen door, and the pain as our eyes locked was immense. Pascal had the good grace to look uncomfortable, but Selma gloated behind his shoulder. I wanted the ground to swallow me whole.

"Liv! I ..." His faltering words elicited a poke in the shoulder from Selma. "I've come to get some of my things."

"He needs his suit, Liv, and something smart casual," Selma crowed. "We're spending next weekend with the Carmichaels at their country pile. We'll be riding to hounds on the Sunday morning." Selma's tone was almost haughty. In other circumstances I would have laughed at her pretentiousness, and so would Pascal. He looked a touch embarrassed as I caught his eye and quickly looked away, motioning to the stairs. "I just need some of my things, Liv," Pascal muttered. "Can I?"

"Sure," I said, unable to keep the anger from my voice. "Help yourself."

"Thanks," he managed to mumble and walked to the stairs. Selma turned to follow.

Words, without thought, shot from my mouth. "No way! No way! No way! Away from the stairs you stay!" The tips of my fingers fizzled, and Selma staggered as the heel of her right stiletto snapped. Arms flailing, she squealed and tumbled, knocking into Pascal as he took the first riser. He thudded to the stairs with a grunt as she landed on his back. At my feet, a voice hissed, 'What have I missed?'

"Shh!" I reprimanded as Lucifer wound himself around my ankles.

"Don't worry," he said with his usual nonchalance as Pascal and Selma untangled themselves and made clumsy efforts to stand, "they can't understand me."

Selma hobbled away from Pascal. "You did it!" she hissed. "It was you!"

"Selma!" Pascal chided. "We've spoken about this." His voice carried a warning, but it was impotent against Selma's rage.

She took another hobbling step, obviously in pain, and jabbed the broken heel at me. "You muttered something, just like at the party, and then I fell."

"I did not!" I lied, summoning as much credibility as I could muster. "It must have been the radio you heard. How can I have caused your heel to snap?"

"You're jealous! I know you hate me."

I stared back at her then, unable to disagree.

"Selma, why don't you go back home," Pascal urged. "Let me get my clothes. I'll be ten minutes."

Selma continued to stare me down and I managed to hold her gaze until she muttered 'Sure' then hobbled from the house, slamming the door behind her.

"God, I hate that woman!" I blurted, unable to suppress my emotion.

"I'll just get my things ..." was Pascal's inept reply and, in that moment, I hated him too.

Ten minutes later he reappeared, a large suitcase packed. With a sombre expression, he hovered at the door for several excruciating moments then broke the silence with, 'She's not a bad person, Liv.'

The heat deep in my belly began to grow and my fingers tingled again.

"Just tell him to leave, Livitha," Lucifer coached. "Before you do something you will regret."

Pascal made no hint that he had heard the cat speak and, with all the self-control I had left, I calmly asked him to leave. A single spark from my index finger shot to the floor as he turned to leave and I closed the door with a sigh of relief, tiny, painful, sparks flying from my hands.

"Dear girl," Lucifer drawled, "do calm down."

After rejecting the idea of a cup of tea, and instead opening a bottle of wine, I spent the next part of the evening scrolling through a poorly written book on witchcraft on my kindle and, as I finished my second glass, devising ridiculous ways of taking revenge on my husband and his lover.

Lucifer licked at the wine placed in a saucer beside him on the sofa, I no longer cared if it became stained. "You could try to turn him into a toad, you know," he said with a wry chuckle then went back to licking the wine.

I wondered if it was possible for cats to get drunk and then said, "Show me."

"No!"

Surprised at his steadfast refusal, I spent the next minutes attempting to change his mind, but he would not budge.

"You must wait for your initiation, Livitha. Those are the rules."

I remembered the two occasions when my emotions had risen to such a peak that sparks had flown from my hands, the numerous days until the Solstice ceremony when I was to be initiated into the coven, and then learn to channel the unpredictable energy that coursed through my body, seemed too far away. I also wanted to change Selma into a toad with far more relish than was seemly for a fifty-year old suburban housewife.

As Lucifer uttered a final, decisive, 'No!' I gave up and returned to my kindle. A chapter titled 'Familiars: their role and purpose' reanimated me. "So, it says here that as my familiar, your role is to be my spy ..." I waited for the laconic response. I wasn't disappointed.

"Tick."

"And a companion ..."

"Correct."

"And ... a domestic servant ..."

With this last statement he pulled his head from the saucer, and stared at me for several moments, before returning to the wine.

"In that case, I'd like you to-"

"Now stop right there!"

I feigned surprise. "Is there something wrong, Lucifer?"

"Well, I am your familiar ..." he sputtered, "and not ... and not your skivvy!"

I laughed. "Don't worry," I said stroking his silky fur for the first time since I'd made the discovery that he could talk. "We can do the laundry on a rota basis." He stiffened, eyed me with huge green eyes filled with as much disdain as he could muster, then jumped off the sofa and stropped out of the room, tail swishing. I chuckled and couldn't help calling after him, "Put the bin out, Lou, they're collecting in the morning." I had no intention of asking my cat to do the housework, but after all the condescending comments and disdainful glares I had received over the last few days, payback felt good.

Chapter Six

The following evening the first indication that something was going on in the street outside my house, was the loud slam of a car door and then a woman hurling abuse as it departed. Unable to sleep, I had stayed up late, kindle on, looking for books about witchcraft and the history of witches. Searching through the pseudo-witchy dross was taking far longer than I had anticipated, although several books were now in my library. Aunt Loveday had promised to lend me some of hers, books that had been written centuries ago, and also promised to introduce me to Ragnhild, a woman she referred to as a warlock. This surprised me as I had assumed that a warlock would be male. Aunt Loveday had then explained that within our community, which could trace its ancestry back to the time before Christianity began to spread among the pagans, a warlock was someone who kept their knowledge safe. 'She is a purist', Aunt Loveday explained, 'and prefers the term Varðlokkur – a keeper of secrets, a caller of spirits. But 'warlock' is what people recognise, and its positive connotations are experiencing a renaissance. The derogatory use of the name to mean a liar, or an oath breaker is just another example of how our people were maligned.'

Placing my kindle on the sofa beside Lucifer, I rose to check the street outside and close the window against the noise. It was unusual for the street to be bombarded with expletives, and was particularly quiet during the evenings, and Mrs. Babcock from across the road was peering out from her bedroom window at the scene.

To my amusement, Selma Maybrook tottered on high heels, staggered, and lurched forward, scraping her hand along the path. As she took another step, her high-heeled shoe cockled, and she continued her journey into the bush at the front of the house with a limp. I snorted my derision. "Come and look at this Lucifer! It's that horrid home-wrecker drunk as a skunk!" I laughed out loud as she made another attempt to walk through her gate. She fell against the privet and stayed there. "Hah! Pascal will not be pleased! He hates it when I have too much to drink. I wonder where he is?"

"Business trip to Dublin," Lucifer replied with nonchalance. "Mrs. Babcock is watching you laugh, Livitha." His words held a hint of disdain. "I'm assuming she's expecting you to become the good Samaritan."

I huffed. Lucifer was right and Marjorie Babcock, another of my uptight holier-than-though neighbours, was staring straight at me. She even gestured to the half-cut figure of Selma Maybrook prone in the privet. "Why should I!" I grumbled. I shrugged my shoulders, raising my hands in a 'what am I supposed to do gesture' to Marjorie. Instead of leaving it, the woman stabbed a finger at Selma. Her meaning was clear; I had to help. "For goodness sake!" I waved at Marjorie to signal my acceptance with as much grace as I could muster, then left the house in high curmudgeon at being forced to help the one woman I swore I would not spit on if she were on fire!

The air was muggy, a summer storm threatened after weeks of unusually hot and sunny weather, and Selma was struggling against the privet, cursing it with language I had never heard falling from another woman's tongue. A foul-mouthed harridan is what my aunts would have called her. She grappled with the hedge as though it were a monster attacking her, swearing like a navvy in slurred, barely decipherable, speech.

"Can I help, Selma?" I asked, watching her car crash efforts at standing, hoping that her drunkenness was an indication of problems between herself and Pascal.

At first, she didn't hear me, but as I repeated my offer of help, noting that Mrs. Babcock was still watching, she turned and stared at me with barely focusing eyes. The woman was completely trollied!

She waved a hand at me which I took as acceptance of my help and pulled her from the privet. The fabric of her silky top snagged, and leaves and twigs remained attached to her hair. The late summer evening light was enough to show that she had been crying; her eyes were panda-like with smudged eyeliner, mascara had run in streams down her cheeks, and lipstick was smeared on her top lip. "What happened?" I asked, my dislike of the woman momentarily displaced by concern that she may have been attacked. "Who was in the car?" She staggered against me, her answer a mumble, and we made our way to her front door. It took several minutes of searching her bag for the front door key, but I managed to find it, entered the house, and deposited her on the sofa. She lay back and began to cry, mascara, still wet, now dripping onto her immaculate cream sofa. I watched her for a moment, noting with satisfaction that she was an ugly crier.

"Swasn't me!" she wailed. "Not me. She shed I did killed S'mon, but twasn't!"

For a moment I couldn't understand what a shed had to do with Simon until my brain translated her alcohol befuddled words. 'It wasn't me! Not me. She said I killed Simon, but it wasn't.' I had no idea who Simon was until she continued.

"I loved Simon," she wailed, snot flowing freely on her top lip. She seemed to sober a little then and sat up, stared directly at me, and said. "His wife's a bitch and he loved me not her!" She descended into sobs again as she wailed, "He was going to leave her, but he didn't have the balls!"

I realised then that she was talking about another man's wife, another marriage she had damaged. Any pity I had for the woman evaporated.

"I see."

"You see ... it wasn't me who killed him, Liv!" She grew silent for a moment then the alcohol took over again. "I love you Liv! Pascal loves you too, but it's my turn you see." The words came out in a slur and she staggered to a stand, slapped her arm across my shoulder then demanded I help her to bed. I should have refused and left her to her own, very drunken, devices, but I couldn't bring myself to be that ignorant so helped her up the stairs and into bed, even removing her high heels and dress then slipping the duvet up to her chin.

She continued to ramble about Simon and how seeing the coffin had broken her heart. "I cried then, in the church, and Sally ... Sally went mental!" As she continued describing the afternoon, I pieced together the scene. Selma had attended the funeral of an ex-lover who had also been a colleague, had become emotional as the casket was carried down the aisle in the church, and caught the attention of the grieving widow who had cast her angry glances for the remainder of the funeral.

Despite not being asked back to the wake, Selma had accompanied some other colleagues, and begun to drink 'to ease the pain'. The widow had taken her opportunity to confront Selma as she had stood outside with her colleagues as they smoked. All hell had broken loose as 'the bitch' had accused her of killing Simon, calling her a 'harlot' and a 'whore', and screaming that she had ruined their marriage. At some point during the tirade, the woman had physically launched herself at Selma and had to be dragged off then carried back inside by three of her colleagues. Mortified, but determined not to leave, she had continued to drink until Sally had again appeared and renewed her tirade of abuse and accusations of murder. It was at this point that a colleague, 'a back-stabbing pig', had taken the initiative and dropped Selma off outside her house. I listened to her drunken ramblings until she passed out then made my way home.

The following morning I woke with a pounding headache, my head filled with bizarre, barely remembered dreams, and bathed in sweat so bad it pooled between my breasts. For once I was glad that Pascal wasn't beside me. After showering and checking for any new hairs that had dared to sprout on my chin and making a mental note to ask the aunts if they had any spells that would stop the wayward growth, I determined to make it my mission to discover a spell that would put a stop to the menopause completely. Whilst we're at it, I thought, why not stop the whole darned ageing process!

As I peered at my chin in the bathroom mirror, spotting a particularly wiry-looking black hair with the help of my reading glasses, I remembered Selma Maybrook. My conscience began to nag; I should check on her. Though resentful at being forced to check on the welfare of the one woman I now detested, I made my way to her house.

After several unanswered knocks, I entered. Everything appeared to be as it had been—immaculate. Selma's house, like her appearance, was perfectly proportioned, and glamorous. I had visited several times, although on most occasions, she would visit us. The difference between our homes was quite marked. I like to be clean and tidy, but my home was, well, homely, and filled with pattern, warm colours, honey-coloured pine, well-worn flagstones, and Persian rugs. In my kitchen, a room often filled with mellow sunlight and a warming glow from the log burner, the windowsill was filled with objects of interest, quirky pieces that had caught my attention. Russian dolls, bird's skulls, fossils, and vintage weighing scales, jostled for position with plants, jars of marbles, an ancient Egyptian canopic jar bought on a holiday to Luxor, and jam jars filled with freshly cut flowers from my garden. Pascal called it clutter, but to me each piece was important. Selma's home was quite different, very modern, and devoid of 'clutter'. The hallway was laid with creamy limestone and led through to a living room with carpets of the lightest grey, complete with a velvet off-white sofa and white walls carefully hung with photographs in silver frames. The images were mainly of herself on various locations with a variety of attractive, obviously wealthy, men and women. Her kitchen, with its minimalist white cupboards and black countertops, was similarly devoid of clutter and nearly any evidence of human occupation.

On the stairs, and marked out by its black frame, hung an award from the newspaper, a piece of investigative journalism she had written a year ago. At the top of the stairs were several rooms including Selma's home office. On my first visit to the house she had shown me around, and I had been amazed at how tidy the office was. There was absolutely nothing out of place and a bookcase against the wall was filled with box files neatly labelled. My collection of files in our home office was chaotic by comparison, the desk littered with papers. Selma was the antithesis to me, and it hurt that Pascal would choose another woman so very different. I thought he had enjoyed my quirkiness, but the realisation dawned that perhaps he had disliked what made me, me, all along.

To my relief, Selma was safely tucked up in bed, but completely dead to the world. Not wanting to disturb her – she would have the most dreadful hangover when she woke – I left, my conscience satisfied.

It wasn't until later, as I went back over the scene in my mind, that I registered that the door of her office had been ajar, and several papers were misaligned on her desk.

Chapter Seven

The days before my initiation were to be spent at our ancestral home and, as the anguish I felt about living beside Pascal and his new girlfriend increased, I decided to leave earlier than planned. My aunts had suggested it, even begged for me to go, so I knew that I would be welcome. I packed with an uneasy mix of sadness and despair bizarrely infused with excitement and had to eventually write a list of every item I needed; my thinking seemed particularly dull today, my memory misfiring.

"Damned menopause!" I muttered, cursing the hormonal imbalances that caused my hot flushes, night sweats, mood swings, and inability to think clearly. And let's not forget those pesky hairs that had decided sprouting from my chin and upper lip was a delightful game! A game of 'pluck' I embraced with the fury of a child playing Whack-a-mole!

Car loaded and ignoring Lucifer as he grumbled from the travel case strapped onto the back seat, I set off for my childhood home, Haligern Cottage. Usually the journey took two hours but as I got stuck behind a wide and very slow tractor for most of the narrow and winding B-road, it took closer to three. Exhausted by the journey I eventually turned off the road and made my way down the narrower driveway that led to the cottage. With the track overhung by trees, I was swallowed into a different realm of tree trunks, ferns and bright green moss bathed in dappled light. At its end, tall wrought iron gates marked the entrance to the house. The surrounding lands, a dense forest that skirted the road for several miles, also belonged to the family; the cottage was a private place, free from prying eyes.

Gates pushed open, I returned to the car and drove into the large turning circle at the front of the house. Calling the house, a cottage, was misleading. With a thatched roof that overhung the small upstairs windows, it certainly looked cottagey, but the original house had spread over the centuries to create a sprawling maze of rooms, and it was nearly as deep as it was wide.

Painted in creamy yellow, with roses growing up over a shingled porch at the front door, it was picturesque in the extreme. I sighed with relief as I stepped out of the car, taking pleasure in its beauty. I had come home. I could finally relax.

Aunts Euphemia and Thomasin met me at the door and I was quickly ushered into the kitchen where my other aunts were busy brewing the tinctures and salves they sold to the locals. Often excitable, Aunt Beatrice seemed particularly on edge as I was offered a cup of tea and told to sit down to rest.

After catching up with some local gossip, the sisters whispered among themselves and then Aunt Beatrice said, "We have some exciting news!" She watched me expectantly but Aunts Thomasin and Loveday looked a little less enthusiastic. Euphemia's excitement was obvious, her eyes glittered with tiny star-like specks in their green irises.

"Well?" I asked, smiling though uncertain; there was an odd tension in the room.

"'We've bought a shop!"

"You and Beatrice have bought a shop," Loveday corrected. The news was the very last thing I expected. "A shop?"

"Yes, yes," Beatrice nodded, unable to contain her excitement and almost dancing as she spoke. "It's in the village," she beamed. "Do you remember Mrs. Duncaster's sweet shop?"

"Yes," I replied, trying to place the shop in my memory. "The one that has been boarded up for the last twenty years!"

"Yes, exactly that one!"

Aunt Loveday barely held back a groan. "Twenty years of collecting dust and growing fungi and wood rot!"

"Oh, it's not that bad, Loveday, and we can fix it up beautifully, just as we have this house."

I looked around the house then. It was certainly true that they kept the house in beautiful condition. They had Mrs. Driscoll for three mornings a week to help with the domestic cleaning, but the fabric of the house itself, despite being centuries old, was in excellent condition without any evidence of damp or sign of wood rot.

Aunt Loveday sighed again. "And you know just how much effort it takes to keep it looking this way, Beatrice."

Beatrice nodded her agreement although a slight frown crossed her brow.

"Everyone can help," Euphemia said with encouragement and Beatrice's face lit up once again.

"I'm sure we can find a local tradesman to help with the renovations, Loveday. We won't have to do anything ourselves," Thomasin added.

It seemed odd to me then that, at over seventy years old, they would consider doing any renovation work themselves, and that got me to wondering who they employed to help with maintaining the cottage. I couldn't remember anyone visiting to make any repairs to the walls, roof, or windows. I viewed the house with clear eyes. The décor had never struck me as odd, it was just my home, but a quick mental scan of the house showed that only my bedroom had wallpaper, and I distinctly remember the aunts decorating the room for me in a 'modern' style as a surprise for my thirteenth birthday. All other walls were whitewashed, or bare stone. The kitchen, with its open hearth, stonework mantel, and large flagstone floor, was ancient. The fireplace was possibly even original to the building, yet it showed no signs of serious deterioration despite constant, pretty much daily, use. Both the heavy outer doors made from solid wood with black ironwork hinges and handles, and the windows, also of black wood with multiple small panes of thick and uneven opaque glass, appeared to be period pieces in pristine condition.

I was about to ask who they employed to help maintain the house when Raif, Aunt Loveday's husband, returned from his walk, a brace of pheasants in hand. His face brightened as he spotted me among the women.

"Livitha! As I live and breathe, you become more beautiful with each passing year!"

Uncle Raif's welcomes were one of the highlights of my visits. The warmth he exuded was like being wrapped in a warm blanket on a cold day. Without embarrassment, I strode across the flagged floor and planted a warm kiss on his bearded cheek. He wore his beard in a distinctive style, quite sharp at the tip and with moustaches pinched at the end. He reminded me of one of the portraits that hung on the gallery landing of an Elizabethan ancestor painted in his finery of ruffed collar, embroidered doublet, fitted hose, and not insignificant codpiece—an item of clothing that teenage Liv had found both hilarious and excruciatingly embarrassing to look at. There was a familiarity of face too, although Uncle Raif's hair was snow white, the Elizabethan gentleman's jet black.

"Hello, Uncle Raif," I said, immediately a girl again. "And you look just as young as last year!" It was true, Uncle Raif looked just the same as he always had ... just exactly the same! I drew back a little and gave his face a quick once over. Although I was unsure of his exact age - he refused to celebrate his birthday - he looked to be just a little older than Aunt Loveday. A sudden desire to question him about his age, his place of birth, his life, and exactly what he was - witch, warlock, or country gent with extremely good genes - was quashed by my inner moral compass; asking would be rude and uncouth, and the very last thing I could bear to be thought of by my very gentlemanly Uncle Raif, was rude and uncouth.

Beatrice nudged me as Uncle Raif disappeared to remove his walking boots and hang the pheasants from that morning's shoot. "He's older than you think!"

"You've been doing it again!" I said with a longsuffering shake of my head.

"Sorry! But you're just so easy to read ... and *interesting*!"

I flushed then and decided to discover a way to block her mindreading.

"Just repeat a mantra when I'm around ... on second thoughts, don't! Listening to the same phrase over, and over again would drive me batty! I wouldn't be the first witch to lose the plot that way you know," she huffed. "Anyway, I digress. He's *much* older than you think. Guess!"

"Oh, I don't know. Erm ... seventy-eight."

"No, no! Be serious. *Much* older."

"I tried again. "Ninety-two?" I said with a shrug of my shoulders.

"More, more!" Her eyes glittered, their violet irises dancing in the light from the mullioned windows.

"More?"

"Yes, yes! She nudged me with her elbow. "Go on, then. Guess!"

I took a wildly high guess. "Four hundred and ninety-one?"

"Hah! Someone told you." She seemed disappointed.

"You can't be serious."

"I am. Oh, yes," she said and then tugged at my sleeve forcing me to bend down to her and whispered. "Fifteen twenty-nine is when he was born, and he met Loveday when he was thirty-two. He was so handsome back then. Oh, a young girl's dream. But then, you've already seen him—on the stairs."

It clicked then why the painting looked so familiar—the Elizabethan gentleman *was* Uncle Raif!

I had so many questions, but at that moment he returned with Loveday on his arm, the epitome of gentlemanly chivalry. "We're taking a turn in the garden. If you'll excuse us, ladies." Beatrice nodded - and I swear she curtsied too - as I offered, 'of course', and they left together to walk in the garden.

"So in love!"

Lucifer strolled to my side then and was joined by Bess, Beatrice's familiar, a slender and finely boned whippet with a coat the colour of a moonless night. The dog's nervous energy matched my aunt's and Lucifer batted at her muzzle as she pushed at his shoulder with her nose. Bess yelped as Lucifer's sharp claws scratched. Within a second both had darted for the door.

"Those two!" Aunt Beatrice said with a laugh. "They love to wind each other up."

The remainder of the day was spent in happy oblivion unpacking my belongings, exploring the grounds, and generally soaking in the rejuvenating atmosphere of Haligern Cottage. I slept fairly well that night, only marred by a few strange dreams, and the next day was enrolled in helping decant the herbal ointments, salves, and moisturising lotions that my aunts sold to the local population in glass jars.

After lunch, I helped wash and prepare herbs from the garden for a lavender tincture the aunts had devised. A large black cauldron hung from an iron chain in the hearth, but Beatrice pulled out a modern aluminium saucepan and placed it on the stove. "It looks the part." She motioned to the blackened cauldron, "but modern pans are so much easier to use."

The herbs washed, chopped, and ground to the aunts' satisfaction, I pleaded a headache and retired to my room. In truth, my mood had shifted down a gear as memories of Pascal and Selma began to dominate my thoughts. I checked my mobile for messages, or missed calls, then lay on the bed, staring at the ceiling like a lovelorn teenager. Beneath the pain of betrayal was something else; I missed my husband and, even surrounded by loving family, I was growing lonely.

As I closed my eyes, a tear slipped down my cheek. And then my mobile rang.

Chapter Eight

My heart jumped to my mouth as I stared at the mobile's screen. Pascal was finally calling! Holding the phone at arm's length as though it would burn if I brought it too close, I accepted the call. "Yes?" My voice was tentative with a slight wobble and I instantly readjusted my tone; I sounded like such a pathetic victim. Without waiting for a reply, I said, "What do you want, Pascal?" Despite my pounding heart, this time my voice was stronger and without that grovelling tone Aunt Loveday had reprimanded me for during our chat in the kitchen. Her voice echoed in my memory. 'You must stand up for yourself, Livitha. You are a strong and independent woman.' I had argued that I had been a housewife for the last twenty-six years and had no idea how to be single, let alone look for work. She had instantly reprimanded me, reminding me of my new powers, powers that had been latent my entire life, and that it was time to embrace them rather than shy away from them. The women of Heligern, she had said, did not live in fear. I took a deep breath as I waited for Pascal to reply, enjoying the sensation of relief that spread through me. 'I am a powerful woman,' I said to myself. 'I am strong, and in control.' *And don't forget that you're also a witch and could turn him into a toad if you wanted.* The thought made me giggle.

"Liv? ... Is that you?"

I struggled with my composure, the image of a green and slimy toad with Pascal's face now bright in my mind.

"Yes," I managed to reply. "It's me."

There was a pause. "Well ... erm ... - *Was he going to make a grovelling apology?* - I don't know how to tell you this but ... - *Was he going to ask me back?* My heart began to pound - but ... you're wanted for murder."

My gasp of fright echoed around the room. "What?" I managed, though my voice was thick in my throat. I realised in that moment that I had believed he was going to ask me back, and the sensation of stupidity was perfectly blended with absolute horror. "Wanted for murder?" I managed. "Murder!"

He sobbed then said, "Yes! The police have been here all day ..." His voice petered out.

The hairs on my arms bristled. "Pascal? ... Pascal, who has been murdered? I don't understand-"

"Selma!" He blurted. "Selma's dead!" He sobbed again, and his pain was obvious.

My anger riled. How dare he feel that much pain about someone he barely knew! I instantly regretted the thought and berated myself for being so insensitive. I sounded callous and shame ran through me. What on earth was going on with my life? "I can't believe it!" I said, struggling to find words. "I only saw her yesterday!" This admission only sent him into another fit of crying. Consumed by the need to comfort him, alongside the annoyance of having to listen to him sobbing as I waited to hear exactly what had happened, I raised my voice and grew stern. "Pascal! Please, pull yourself together and tell me exactly why Selma has anything to do with me?"

"She's dead!"

"Yes, we've already established that!"

"She's dead and you were seen leaving the house yesterday morning."

Dawning dread washed over me. "But she was asleep when I left!"

"The police said she died during the early morning. And ... and Mister Grayson has given a statement that he overheard you threaten to kill her!" Pascal began to sob again.

Mr. Grayson, our extremely nosey next-door neighbour, was notoriously anal about watching the CCTV footage from the numerous cameras on his property, patrolling the street as head of the local Neighbourhood Watch group, and a terrible eavesdropper. I knew that he wasn't fond of me, or Pascal, particularly after we found him snooping at the boundary between our properties. My hand began to tremble. "That's insane! I didn't kill her! She was alive when I left. She was!" The line grew quiet. "You do believe me, Pascal? Don't you?" The mumble from the other end of the line was non-committal and I felt betrayed all over again. "You can't possibly think ..." My voice trailed off.

"I've given the police your telephone number, Liv. I just wanted to warn you ... so you could get your story straight."

Get my story straight! "What? Pascal, I ... I didn't do it."

He made a pathetic bubbling noise then the phoneline went dead. I glanced at the blank screen then threw the phone on the bed as though scalded. At any second it would ring, and the police would accuse me of murder!

After pacing my room for the next half an hour expecting the telephone to ring with each passing second, I made my way downstairs and found my aunts in the orangery enjoying their afternoon tea. It took several minutes before I had the courage to tell them about Pascal's phone call. The fact that he appeared to have a question about my innocence had rocked my confidence.

"You didn't, did you?" Aunt Euphemia asked as I relayed my conversation with Pascal.

"No! Of course not!"

"Do you think it's the curse?"

"No, we countered it immediately," Aunt Loveday said. "It would have no effect, or at least be weakened to near impotence."

"I hope so!"

"Livitha's powers are particularly strong ... Pascal could be next!" There was a note of joy in Aunt Beatrice's voice.

Pascal could be next!

"Don't be silly, Beatrice. She uttered the curse in a moment of great perturbation." Aunt Loveday eyed me steadily as though weighing up the truth of her statement. "No, I'm sure it could not have been the curse." There was a quiver of uncertainty in her voice and even I began to have my doubts.

They had me believing in my power to curse now! "Do you really think it was me?"

"No, of course not, darling."

"Perhaps not intentionally, but ..."

I panicked. "Of course, I didn't kill the woman! I helped to put her to bed when she was drunk—that's all. When I left the house, she was still breathing, snoring even!"

"Don't get overexcited, dear," Aunt Thomasin soothed. "It could have been natural causes. Sad-"

"Yes, she was kind of sad, well beside herself really," I readily agreed. If she had taken her own life, then I couldn't be to blame.

"No! S.A.D.S. Sudden Adult Death Syndrome. She just died in her sleep."

"That's how they often die when cursed," Aunt Beatrice added.

"Bee! You're not helping."

"Sorry! Well ... perhaps she died in her own vomit? Livitha did say that she was in an alcoholic stupor."

All four aunts pulled a grimace.

"What a horrid way to go!"

"Very messy."

"Nasty!"

"I don't think she was *that* drunk!" I interjected. "I mean, she could still talk. She was lucid enough to whine about the funeral she had just been to, and how much she had loved the dead man, and that it wasn't her fault he had died despite what his wife said."

"Ooh! Sounds intriguing. Tell me more."

"I don't know any more than that. She had been to the funeral of an ex-lover and been confronted by the wife-"

"Denizen!"

"Because she said something about it not being her fault that he died, I'm guessing the wife blamed her for his death."

"And how did he die?"

"I'm not sure. A lot of what Selma said was rambling and indecipherable. She was certainly very unhappy. I thought that she would wake up with a stinking hangover!"

"Instead, she woke up dead!"

"Oh, Euphemia! How could she have possibly woken up dead?"

Euphemia laughed, realising her flawed logic. "Well, of course she didn't wake up dead, although I know a few people who have." All four aunts laughed.

"One very memorable count for certain!"

"Vlad? Yes, he certainly got more than he bargained for. Silly man. Just shows that you really shouldn't dabble with dark magick and make pacts with forces that should never be invoked!"

"Most certainly true, Loveday."

My head reeled. Now that I had been made aware of our witchy status, my aunts' conversations flowed far more freely and were peppered with hints at so much intriguing and fascinating history. It made sense now why their words had always seemed to be so carefully chosen and deliberate, and the numerous occasions when one had given the other a sharp glance to quiet them. Intrigued, I had to ask the question. "Are you talking about Vlad the Impaler?"

"No, no darling. Vlad the Vampire."

"They're the same person, Euphemia," Aunt Loveday confirmed.

"You *would* know him as Count Dracula though, dear," Aunt Thomasin explained. "Really, a very sad case."

"Sad? He died in his sleep?"

"Well ... not that kind of sad dear, but yes, he slipped this mortal coil in his sleep. What I meant was that he was an emotional wreck. He lost his soulmate and couldn't bear to walk the earth without her so he made a deal with the darker forces - he that shall not be named - so that he could walk the shadows to find her soul." Aunt Loveday clasped Raif's hand as Thomasin talked of Vlad's lost soulmate and they exchanged a private, knowing glance.

"... and the rest is history."

"Is he still living in New Orleans?"

"No, I don't think so. The last I heard he had moved to New Zealand. Wellington, I think. Poor man has to keep moving around to keep his identity secret."

"Yes, poor man. Just look at what happened in Salem!"

"Those girls should never have invited him to stay."

"The way those locals treated him, and Igor, was just terrible."

"Perhaps we should invite him over? He could be our summer guest this year."

Aunt Loveday coughed. "I think last summer was quite exciting enough for one decade," she said without elaboration. "This summer is all about Livitha."

"Of course."

"As it should be."

"Indeed."

I sat in confusion, desperate to know exactly what happened last summer, but still grappling with the idea that the witches of Salem had invited a vampire to stay, and that the count had been, at one point, a resident of New Orleans. My head spun as I remembered images from television shows and films: David Soul as the writer discovering the foul vampire living in Salem's Lot, Tom Cruise as the vampire L'Estat, and Brad Pitt as Louis de Pointe du Lac.

"I know what you're thinking, Livitha, and yes those books were inspired by his life."

"Did you just read my mind?" I asked, scorched by Aunt Beatrice's words.

"No, of course not!"

I stared at her. Aunt Loveday's lips pursed. "Beatrice?"

"Well, just a little."

"Oh, Beatrice, you really mustn't."

"I know, but it's so hard not to hear her! Her force is so great."

"That's as may be, but it really is an intrusion. The girl has a right to privacy—as do we all."

Aunt Beatrice's cheeks flushed as though she were a naughty schoolgirl. Feeling awkward for her, I said, "It's okay, Aunt Bee. It's my fault."

"Obviously, it is not, Livitha, but we'll drop the subject now. Anyway," Aunt Loveday continued, "Beatrice is quite correct; those books were inspired by the Count, but obviously events were ... manipulated ... to suit the writer's needs and make a great story."

I remembered the hideous vampire depicted in Stephen King's novel. "The Count ... what does he look like?"

"Ooh!" exclaimed Aunt Thomasin. "He is absolutely stunning!"

"So ... not a Nosferatu kind of vampire then?"

"No, no. That type are quite a different breed. No, Count Vlad is much more Christopher Lee than those fetid animals."

"He does rather remind me of Gary Oldman in 'Dracula.'"

I shuddered, remembering the repulsive white-haired and wrinkled monster. "But he was grotesque in that!"

"Oh, no! I mean the younger Dracula; the one Winona fell in love with."

My relief was palpable. The thought of having some hideous vampire stalking the halls during the night for the entirety of the summer was too much to contemplate.

Again, I found it hard to process the information. I had so many questions, but they would have to wait. The conversation turned again to the telephone call I had received from Pascal.

"So, the police are looking for you?"

"Well ... yes. The neighbour, Mister Grayson, has apparently told them that he saw me leaving the scene – Selma's house – first thing in the morning, and they want to question me to eliminate me from their enquiries." As I said this, the hairs on my neck stood on end. I had seen enough crime dramas on television to know that anyone leaving the scene was a prime suspect. That I had also threatened to kill the woman the previous week, only added to my condemnation. "Well, what Pascal actually said is that they want me for murder!"

A communal hiss filled the room.

After several moments Aunt Beatrice said, "Well, she can't turn herself in. We have far too many guests arriving for the Solstice and they're all expecting to see Liv."

Aunt Loveday nodded, her face deadly serious. "You're right, Bee. It would be a terrible insult to them if she were not to make an appearance." She turned to me then. "It's imperative that you're here, Livitha! We have so many important guests coming. The perceived insult if you were not to be here to greet them, would be dreadful. It could take decades of work for us to put things right."

"Maybe centuries!"

"I won't answer the phone then," I offered.

"Good girl."

"So ..." I couldn't help a sly smile. "I'll be an outlaw?"

"Well, I guess you will be."

"What a rebel!" Aunt Euphemia joked.

In the next moment, the telephone rang. The print on the screen read, 'Unknown Number'.

Chapter Nine

The constant ringing of the phone was the only noise in the room. When it stopped, my aunts breathed a collective sigh of relief. I considered removing the battery so that the phone wouldn't ring again, but decided against that; turning the mobile off would be like swimming in the dark, and I wanted to know when, and how often, the police tried to contact me. It crossed my mind that Pascal may have given more information away than just my telephone number.

"What if they come here? Pascal may have given them the address. He knows that if I'm not at home overnight, here is the most likely place I'll be."

All four aunts stared at me then exchanged glances.

"We'll hide you! There are so many nooks and crannies in this old place."

"The witch hole!"

"No, Euphemia, she wouldn't fit!"

"Of course she would, Bee! She's not that ... fat."

The familiar stinging rose to my cheeks.

"That's not what I meant," Beatrice said quickly although her glance from me to the floor told me otherwise. I decided in that moment to do something about the extra weight I had accumulated in the past ten years. Perhaps there was a spell? Something to lock my jaws together, or something that would reduce my appetite and stop me craving sugar when my world was a little wobbly? "Lockjaw!" Beatrice whispered and, from the way she clamped her lips together, I knew that she had read my mind again.

Aunt Loveday threw Beatrice another disapproving frown then said, "I'm sure that hiding Livitha in witches' holes, isn't necessary. The police will need a warrant to search the house, and I doubt, at this stage of the investigation, that they will have that.

At this stage of the investigation! "Do you really think they'll want to search the house for me?"

"Well, in our experience," Aunt Loveday glanced at the gathered women, "which, I'm sad to say, goes back through very many centuries of persecution, when one of us comes under suspicion the hunters invariably demand to search the house." She said this with such gravity that a chill ran down through my arms and tingled at my fingertips. Heat began to accumulate in my core. Annoyed at this hormonal hijacking of my body, I tried to control it; now was not the time for a menopausal hot flush. However, the heat grew like a fiery ball and rose to my chest. Sweat seemed to be gathering at my temples and the sensation of tiny electric shocks ran down my arms to the tips of my fingers.

"Liv!" Aunt Thomasin called. "Be careful!" She jabbed a finger at my hands. Sparks crackled at my fingertips, and minute particles struck the floor. Tiny trails of smoke rose from the Persian rug.

"Sorry!" I gasped, immediately stamping on the carpet whilst staring at my hands in horror.

"That's silk, and two hundred years old!"

Anxiety burst inside me and the fizzing in my fingers became painful. "I can't stop it!"

"Oh, for the love of Thor!"

"Outside!" Aunt Thomasin urged. "Get her outside." Whilst I was overridden with fear and anticipation at the fizzing power building in my fingertips, wild excitement glittered in Aunt Thomasin's eyes. "She's gonna blow!"

"We haven't given her guidance, Loveday!" Aunt Euphemia's voice was laced with trepidation.

"Let's just get her outside!"

Fingertips sparking, I was bundled through the house and out into the garden. Placed at a safe distance from the house, and with the heat in my body set to 'spontaneous combustion', my aunts took several steps back.

"You can let it go now, Liv!"

"Just aim at the compost heap," instructed Euphemia.

"The compost heap is too close to the shed."

"Or the grass, then," Euphemia corrected.

"No, not the grass. It's so dry. We've had no rain for weeks."

"Okay. The compost heap, then."

"Just throw it out!"

"Make sure to think of something nice!"

"We should have warned her about this!"

"Remiss of us not to!"

"This could be a catastrophe!"

"Tell her to think of something nice!"

"Sisters!" Aunt Loveday reprimanded.

Confused, overwhelmed by the heat and sensation of electricity coursing through my body, and the anxiety rising among my aunts, I dithered, pointing my arms out towards the compost heap, the shed, and the grass, and then flung them at the bank of trees that surrounded the house, fronted by an ancient oak.

"No, Liv! Not the oak!"

Too late, the power that had built inside me escaped with such force that the air around us vibrated, crackled, and sparked, and every ounce of that energy landed on the tree. A collective gasp was lost in the explosion of energy that followed.

The tree shivered and seemed to writhe. It was as though it came alive and, for several seconds, I thought that it would uproot and step forward. Instead, its branches became arm-like, waving rhythmically as its trunk swayed, and it reminded me of a belly dancer. With a final terrifying shiver, it stopped, and then a single creamy sphere grew from an acorn low in its branches.

"What is that?" Aunt Euphemia asked as the sphere continued to grow.

Too drained to move, I watched the globe, Aunt Loveday at my side. "Watch, Liv. I think something special is about to happen. It has been such a long time since I saw it last."

A transformation took place that I will remember for the rest of my life. The globe continued to grow until it was the size of an orange, deepening from white to a creamy pale pink. Then, incredibly, it began to open, revealing petal after petal. "It's a ... peony!" I gazed at the huge and perfectly cupped bloom.

"Is it the 'nice' thing you thought of?"

"I guess so. It's all such a blur, but my garden did flash in my mind for a moment ... I think."

What followed was incredible. Each acorn on the tree transformed into a globe, grew, and bloomed. Over the next ten minutes, we stood in awe, watching the ancient oak blossom with peony-like flowers. It was so burdened by the blooms that I feared its boughs would break.

"That is incredible."

"Truly awesome."

"Fantastical. I have never seen anything like it."

"I have seen it once, but not since Leofrun of Lindsey."

"I'm not familiar with her."

"Years before your time, darling, but one of my closest allies back in the day."

"Ahh. I'd like to meet her."

"Sadly, she lost her life after the battle of Wodensfield. She foretold of the Danish defeat, and Healfdene's widow had her executed. She believed that it was Leofrun's witchcraft that had brought about Healfdene's death."

"Terrible."

"Yes, quite horrible."

"I'm so glad those days are over!"

"I wish they were, darling."

As aunt Loveday continued to reminisce about her past, I wondered at quite how old she was and watched as the blooms began to fall. Thousands of petals, picked up by the breeze, floated down onto the grass and then faded to nothing. Within another ten minutes, all evidence that the phenomenon had ever happened, was gone.

Back in the house, we sat at the well-scrubbed kitchen table, surrounded by Aunt Beatrice's drying herbs. When cooking wasn't in progress, the room held an aroma of lavender and bay leaf with another, unidentified odour of something slightly acrid. This morning, the day's bright sunshine cast its rays across the table, warming my hands which had become cold and pale after my 'outburst' of energy.

"What we must do, with some urgency," Aunt Loveday explained, "is to teach you how to control your emotions."

"If that outburst was anything to go by, then the girl's a wreck!"

"Euphemia! That's not helpful."

"She's hormonal. The menopause is a powerful time in a witch's life."

"Indeed, it is, which is why those of us who are blessed come into our powers at that time."

"At least in our line."

"Do other women 'come into power' at other times?"

"Yes, they do, but we'll get back to that; we need to deal with the current crisis."

"The murder?" Aunt Thomasin had an excited twinkle in her eyes.

"Yes, Thomasin, the murder."

"If the police come here, Livitha can hide."

"We can cast a spell of invisibility."

"Perhaps, but we all need to conserve our energy for the Solstice and Liv's initiation."

The women nodded in murmured agreement.

"I'm not guilty, you know."

"We know," all four voices answered with varying degrees of soothing and earnest sympathy.

"What if they do turn up here with a search warrant?"

"I'm sure they won't, Liv."

"What if they turn up with an arrest warrant? Pascal seemed sure they wanted me for murder! They wouldn't say that unless they were certain."

"I don't believe they said that at all!"

"Those were the words Pascal used."

Loveday sighed.

"If they turn up with an arrest warrant, they could take her into custody and then our Solstice will be ruined."

"As will her initiation."

"You know it's her only chance of joining the coven. She must join at this point in her cycle otherwise she will never attain the power she is capable of."

Loveday murmured but remained tight-lipped.

"I'm going back!" I said with sudden clarity. "I'm going back to find out who *did* kill Selma."

"But what about the Solstice?"

"I'll make sure I'm back for that."

"You must!"

"Oh, Liv, how can you possibly discover who killed Selma?"

"Well, given that I'm the prime suspect, I can't do a worse job than the police!"

Despite my aunt's protests, I packed my bag, and within twenty minutes was saying my goodbyes with a solemn promise of returning for the Solstice. As Aunt Loveday opened the door, and I stepped onto the front steps, an unfamiliar car rolled to a stop in the driveway.

Chapter Ten

"It's them!" I stood frozen as the car, an unremarkable but shining blue Lexus, pulled up in front of the house. I knew from Pascal's obsession with spotting unmarked police cars and speed traps that the vehicle would be less than three years old, be purchased from a major manufacturer in pristine condition, and be clean. It would perhaps be loaded with 'kit' on the dashboard, and maybe low at the back due to the 'gear' they had to carry. I was uncertain what the 'kit' or 'gear' would be, as Pascal had never elaborated, but the two people in the front seats, a man and a woman, wore the same serious expression and dark suits that I imagined of police detectives. The big giveaway of these nondescript cars, Pascal had said, were the hidden LEDs tucked behind the grille, placed so that they didn't give the game away like multiple aerials used to, but available so that they could 'flash the blues' if they needed to get somewhere in a hurry, or chase a speeding motorist. Spotting the LED lights tucked behind the grille, I wondered if the pair had the lights flashing blue when they set off to capture me.

Half-hidden by the sunshield, the man reached for the dashboard, retrieved a handheld radio, and spoke into it as the woman held up a sheaf of paper. Paranoia set in, and I imagined the paper was a list of their evidence against me, much of it supplied by Mr. Grayson and Mrs. Babcock, nosey neighbours who must have heard the commotion on the night of the party when the guests had been entertained by angry shouts and accusations of infidelity and revenge. Perhaps they had even heard the argument in the hallway where Selma had screamed that I hated her. Being seen leaving the house on the morning of the murder sealed the deal, and I understood why they wanted to question me. But Pascal had said that I was 'wanted for murder' which I guessed meant they had no other suspects to pin it on, and plenty of damning evidence against me. During the past hours I had mulled it over and realised why. I had been the last to see her before she died (apart from the murderer) and the first to see her afterwards. My DNA would be in the house, up her stairs, and in her bedroom. She had even managed to scratch me as I struggled to help her into bed, so my DNA would be underneath her fingernails too. Plus, she had managed to injure herself as we'd lurched through the house, and at one point had fallen on the stairs and knocked her forearms, which could, and I had seen it happen on the television, be seen as defensive bruising! There was also the grazing and injuries she had sustained whilst grappling with the privet and tarmacked path before I went to her aid. I dry swallowed, certain now that the female officer was reeling off each point of evidence against me and the male was radioing Control to confirm that they were about to bring in the 'perp'.

"Go back inside girls," Aunt Loveday instructed. "Livitha, stand behind me and don't speak. Let me deal with this."

"But I should hide!" I said, the urge to run immense.

"No, just stand behind me. I'll take care of them if you'll just follow my instructions."

My aunts disappeared back into the shadow of the hallway as I stood behind Aunt Loveday on the steps. The sun, already bright, was warming the day quickly, but it was the now familiar hot flush that was making me sweat. I took deep breaths in an effort to calm myself; exploding with anxiety-driven energy, as I had done in the garden, would be disastrous right now.

"Stay calm, Liv," Loveday soothed, obviously aware of my growing discomfort. "Everything will be alright."

As the two officers stepped out of the car an ember of heat, deep in my core, began to glow, and electricity shot from my index fingers, sparking on the flagstones. I took another breath, then stared in wonder at the male officer. He was intensely familiar.

"Livitha, when I tap my thigh, I want you to walk to your car and leave."

"But they'll see me!" I managed, staring at the man as he scanned the front of the house, seemingly oblivious to our presence. My mind reeled as he exchanged words with the woman. She laughed in response, and both stepped away from the car in unison and converged at its front. "Garrett Blackwood!" I blurted, unable to hold back my surprise. Not since my teenage years had my heart and belly flipped in such queasy unison as they did at that moment. Garrett Blackwood! My first love, who, as a man, was even more handsome. My breath caught in my chest as I was thrown back into teenage angst, experiencing those intense emotions like a shot of adrenaline straight to my heart. "Garrett!" I took a step forward, but my way was instantly blocked as Aunt Loveday raised her arm, a barrier as strong as a bar of steel.

"A Blackwood!" she whispered.

"Yes! Garrett Blackwood."

Still unaware of our presence, it wasn't until Garrett was about to place his foot on the first flagstone that Aunt Loveday tapped her thigh. I remained still, mesmerised by the sight of the boy, now a man, I had adored as a teenager. Taller than I remembered, he must be at least six-foot-four and broad-chested with it. He had filled out well, with only a hint of middle-age spread. His face, though lined with age, was still chiselled, his nose straight with a slight flare at the nostrils, his lips full and soft, and I realised that he reminded me of Tom Hardy! I was instantly relieved that he couldn't see the less than statuesque greying, mousy-blonde I had become.

My gaze wandered to his hands; his ring finger was bare! Joy infused chaotically with terror and my cheeks burned with heat.

"Go now, Livitha!" Aunt Loveday instructed.

Garrett took another step closer, completely unaware that we were less than three feet apart.

"Go to your car now, Livitha," Loveday instructed.

There was only a narrow gap between Garrett and the rose arch over the door. I would have to slide past him to escape.

"There's the knocker," the policewoman said as Garrett faltered on the step.

With a quizzical frown, he tried to step forward but stopped, his face only two feet from mine. "Liv?"

I gasped as he said my name although he stared right past me to the door.

"Go on then," the policewoman urged. "Knock!"

Aunt Loveday's voice became stern. "Livitha, you must leave now. Take courage and leave. He is a Blackwood, and I can't hold him back for much longer."

Unaware of quite why Garrett being a 'Blackwood' had any significance, I took a step past Aunt Loveday and then side-stepped Garrett. My hand brushed his as I passed, and the sensation was electric. He flinched in response but, with my aunt urging me onwards, I continued past Garrett and the oblivious policewoman, and ran to my car.

As the engine burst into life, Garrett and his colleague stepped beneath the rose arch and knocked on the door. It opened to Aunt Loveday bearing a broad and innocent smile. As I drove away from the house without either police officer showing any sign of having seen or heard the car, Garrett stepped into my ancestral home for the first time in thirty-three years.

I only made it two miles before I had to pull over and gather my senses. My driving had been distracted, and a tractor, then an oncoming car, had caught me unawares on the narrow country road. Pulling into a passing-place, I switched off the engine and bowed my head to rest on the steering wheel, my nerves in tatters. Garrett Blackwood had been my first true love, but more than that, he had been the love of my life. My grief about Pascal paled into insignificance in comparison to the emotional storm that rolled over me as the memories of being torn from my soulmate infused each cell of my body just as intensely as they had at the time. Shocked at the intensity of my feelings, I allowed myself to sit until the nagging concern that perhaps Garrett would pass this way once he had finished at the house forced me to move.

With renewed concern, I started the car and continued my journey back to town. I had to focus! Discovering who killed Selma so that I could clear my name and be free to attend my Solstice initiation had to be my priority. And, if I couldn't discover the murderer, then I had to at least evade being captured. My only experience of the police and crime came from watching dramas on the television, and those detectives didn't give up until they'd caught their man! Or, in this case, woman!

Determined to clear my name, and be free to attend the Solstice, I continued my onward journey, making my best efforts to push thoughts of Garrett Blackwood to the back of my mind, and focus on Selma's murder.

Chapter Eleven

O ne of the few things I knew about police work was that all murder investigations, at least the ones I had viewed on television, started with the scene of the crime. With that in mind, pushing out the paranoid fantasy that my number plate would be logged, and my progress from the house and through town tracked by a multitude of speed cameras, I made my way to Selma's house.

Realising that parking outside the house would be a terrible rookie mistake, I parked the car on an ordinary street at the edge of town, found the pocket-sized torchlight in my roadside bag, and slipped on the dark raincoat and brimmed hat I kept in the boot for emergency purposes. Pulling the brim of the hat down, and ready to begin my quest of discovery, I took a slow walk to the town centre.

At half-past four, I purchased a notebook and sat in a small café drinking coffee and thought through everything I knew about Selma and the events of the evening before her murder then jotted them down, along with notes of evidence, as a series of bullet points:

- Age – 39?
- Degree in English and Criminal Justice from Hull University. MA in Journalism?

- Hometown – Hull.
- ~~Investigative Journalist~~ Redtop hack!
- Home wrecker. Evidence = dead man's wife accused her of ruining marriage. Physical assault at funeral. Pascal.
- Black widow. Evidence = Inheritance from death of first husband (sugar daddy?). Adult children from his first marriage angry (Helen and Derek?). Conversation in kitchen about contested will and accusations her fault he died. Gloating that she won the case and accusations were dismissed.
- Gold digger. Evidence = fortune earned through three lucrative divorces. Made joke in kitchen about how husband 2 (Maynard Montague?) was 'spitting feathers' about having to pay a monthly allowance.
- Problems at work. Evidence = called colleague who dropped her off 'back-stabbing pig'.

I re-read the list with satisfaction. There were at least four people on it who actively hated Selma, and any one of them could have murdered her.

As I finished my coffee and added a few more details to my list, the café closed, and I was asked to leave. Surprised that the time was now six o'clock, I made slow progress through the town then waited until it was dark enough to walk onto my street, staying close to the shadows cast by multiple privet hedges. Some were clipped and angular, whilst others were towering and uncut, but all were grown tall enough to give the houses and their front gardens some privacy from the road. This would give me an advantage; once I was inside the house, it was unlikely that any neighbours would be aware of my presence.

Selma's house, typical of the others in the street, had a generous front garden, fronted by the obligatory enormous privet hedge, with a driveway at the side. Access to the back of the house was blocked by a brick wall with wrought iron gate. Despite the privet hedging, and the growing dark, I decided that entering the house via my own garden would be the best option.

Light shone from my own home. Taken aback, I realised it must be Pascal. Of course he would be back at home rather than in the dead woman's house, and the place where she had been murdered. Since his phone call, and the bombshell he'd dropped, I hadn't given him a second thought. Stepping onto my driveway, I jumped behind the privet and crouched to see through the front window. The curtains were drawn back, and light shone through the darkness from the kitchen where I presumed Pascal would be sitting at the table with a glass of wine, or black coffee growing cold, and his laptop open, oblivious to the real world—as usual.

Taking quiet steps to the back of the house, I searched the garden for a point where I could most easily climb over the boundary hedge. Like many homeowners along the road, the need for privacy meant hedging and fencing marked the boundaries, fences and hedges over which I could not see, fences and hedges that were eight feet high in places. The only way into Selma's garden without breaking my neck was to climb an old apple tree whose bough reached out over her lawn, or a part of the fence that looked rather weak.

I climbed the tree.

Dropping over to the other side, congratulating myself on my newly discovered ninja skills, I reached the back door, breathless, hands scratched, biceps and forearms aching, and legs trembling. Perhaps 'ninja skills' wasn't quite the right description for my efforts, but I had made it, broken no bones nor alerted Pascal to my presence. It was a win, win situation. Above, a bat swooped over the lawn and I ran to the back door, holding an arm above my head to protect my hair. From past conversations, I knew where the spare key for the back door was kept. Creeping along the back of the house, I retrieved the key from under its pot, and let myself in.

The house was deathly quiet, my breath loud and rasping as it echoed in the spacious kitchen, the noise bouncing off the hard and shiny surfaces. A chill ran over me; this was no longer a house, it was a murder scene, and a most heinous crime had taken place directly above my head in Selma's bedroom. It wasn't the first crime committed in that space, but it was the first one with deadly consequences! As the chatter in my head began to sound like a voiceover from an action film trailer, I scanned the kitchen. Movement outside the window caught my eye and I let out a tiny squeal, frozen to the spot. The movement came again, and I realised with relief it was just the bat swooping over the garden, probably in its efforts to catch the insects that swarmed at twilight. The bright moonlight was a contrast to the darkness in the kitchen and the bat swooped among the silhouettes of garden trees. It swooped again, hovered at the window, then disappeared. For a moment I wondered if it was the same bat that had flapped mercilessly overhead on my birthday, but quickly dismissed the thought and turned back to the kitchen, heart pounding, determined to search for any clues.

My first thoughts were to visit the crime scene itself but, as I climbed the stairs, inspecting each neatly framed photograph and the award for journalistic excellence, I baulked at the idea and instead made my way to the office. Despite my dislike of Selma, I found it hard to be in the house knowing that the last time I had stood here the woman had been dead. I shivered, hurried past the open bedroom door with its empty bed, and walked into the office.

The mis-aligned papers I had subconsciously noted on the morning of the murder were still on the floor. Shining the torch around the room, I recognised other signs of disarray in Selma's OCD-level tidy office. Several box files had been moved, and papers had been fanned out on the floor. One of the desk drawers was partially open.

Crouching down to read the papers, I scanned the contents, careful to only touch them with the edge of my coat sleeve. Several of them were printed copies of emails that Selma had been sent (wasteful!) whilst others were handwritten notes. The notes seemed to pertain to various investigative projects Selma was working on, the emails were foul-mouthed rants from someone who hadn't left a signature. The printout showed the email to come from e.d.devon at a company named Naztexholdings.org. I was unfamiliar with the company name, but it was obvious from the content of the email that Selma was despised by the sender, as at least two of his, or her, messages offered threats against her person. Other emails were also threatening, but these only sought legal action against Selma. Another, from a sixth sender made no threats, but defamed her in the most heinous terms. The unfolding picture of Selma's activities and personality was one far more poisonous than I had imagined. Quite why the police hadn't taken these as evidence was hard to understand, unless they were particularly incompetent in this part of the country.

Next, I turned my attention to the box files. Several were out of line. I checked through these first. One labelled 'Mantel/ Frampton Rd.', and another labelled 'Heargholtsby Hill /Gaz-conOG/Schofield'. Each was filled with handwritten notes, newspaper cuttings, and photographs. They were obviously the collection of evidence accumulated for each of Selma's investigations. The published pieces were well-written, erudite, entertaining, and in-depth. Selma obviously had a talent for writing and sniffing out a good story. The evidence that some of her work contributed towards court cases came from another box where a newspaper clipping detailed the guilty verdict of a case Selma had researched and where she had been a witness for the prosecution. Despite my prejudice, I began to admire the man-eating denizen. The woman was certainly more than the 'red-top hack' that I had supposed.

Turning from the bank of box files – it would take days to sift through them – I focused on the desk which had three drawers. The top drawer held nothing more than the usual office stationery of pens, erasers, and paperclips, whilst the second held neat stacks of empty notebooks. However, in the third, was a hardbound accounts book. On lifting it out, I found a manila file taped to its back.

"Aha!"

As I began to peel the tape back and attempt to remove the folded card from the book, a noise from somewhere in the house caught my attention. Senses on edge, my thoughts flew immediately to the bedroom and the image of Selma prone on the bed. The thought of her dead body sent spiky chills tingling down my spine. *She's not in the house! Calm down!* Heart pounding, the follicles of my hair prickling as they stood on end across my scalp, I listened to the noise. It was coming from inside the house! Someone was downstairs.

Chapter Twelve

Heart pounding, the familiar heat beginning to burn in my core as anxiety re-lit the hormonal embers of a full-on hot flush, I stared through the door to the greyed-out landing and listened. The noise seemed to be coming from the kitchen, and the draft that reached the room from downstairs proved that the back door had been opened. Certain that I had closed the door on entry, I took a step away from the desk, fingernail still hooked in the sticky tape holding the manila envelope to the book.

Downstairs, a glass chinked, and footsteps padded across the floor. I dry swallowed. My fingers fizzed as an electrical current began to build, along with the heat at my core. As the intruder downstairs took the first riser on the stairs, there were two things I knew I had to do. One, hide. And two, control the uncontrollable, and stop the hormonal hijacking of my body.

I switched off the torch and stepped with a light foot to the far corner of the room, squeezing myself in between a shelving unit and the wall. A full-length curtain at the window would help to hide me, providing I could stop the rustling of my raincoat, which now seemed thunderous, and the rising heat in my body which was causing my fingertips to spark. Sweat gathered at my hairline. To quell the rising tide of hormonal overload, I took slow breaths through my nose whilst silently repeating the mantra that I was 'calm and in control'.

Whoever was coming up the stairs reached the landing.

Footsteps padded to the open office door. Hardly daring to breathe in case the rustle from my coat, or the sound of my breath, alerted the intruder to my presence, I stood absolutely still. After several moments of silence, it became obvious that whoever stood on the landing wasn't coming into the office and I peered into the room from my hiding place.

The space was dark apart from a sliver of moonlight shining in through a gap in the curtains. As the silence continued, I began to wonder if I had imagined the footsteps on the stairs, and if hallucinations were also a symptom of the menopause. I was about to step out of my hiding place when movement at the door stopped me in my tracks.

As a head peered from behind the open door, I held back a gasp of horror. Two luminous orbs shone out from the dark.

"Liv?"

A familiar voice called my name, and I realised that the creepy orbs were Lucifer's moonlit eyes.

"Lucifer! You frightened me half to death," I exclaimed, stepping out from the corner and shining torchlight at him, relieved to illuminate the darkness. His eyes glinted in the light and he let out a small hiss.

"Get the light out of my eyes, Livitha!"

"Sorry!" I said, still whispering. "But you frightened me. What are you doing here?"

"Pssht! Not much of a witch are you, if a cat can frighten you half to death."

I ignored the insult. "So, it was you making all that noise downstairs!"

"Well, you left muddy footprints across the kitchen floor and I slipped on the tiles. I am not happy. It's clay rich soil around here, you know, and that nasty stuff sticks horribly in my fur and between my toes."

"What are you doing here, Lucifer? I left you back at the cottage!"

"I couldn't let you go out alone."

I smiled at this. "So, you do care."

"Not in the least! I'm here to protect the reputation of the coven. If word gets out about your shenanigans, then we'll be a laughingstock."

"I'm really not sure I like you! You're mean!"

The cat huffed and stalked into the room. "It's been a long day," he complained.

I took that as the closest to an apology I would get for his rudeness, and began to explain about the box files with their meticulous research and the numerous threatening and insulting emails, and then produced the book with the small manila file still stuck to the back.

Keen to discover the contents of the manila file, I scratched at the tape holding it in place. "This could be evidence, Lucifer," I said. "It could lead us to the real killer."

He tutted and shook his head but maintained a steady gaze on the book as I struggled with the tape. After several moments, he said, "Here, let me help," and extended a paw then a claw, and made an incision that cut through the tape perfectly. He was about to make a further incision on the other side of the file when footsteps on the staircase startled us both.

Within an instant Lucifer transformed into a tiny black mouse. I barely held back a scream of revulsion as he scrambled up my leg and disappeared into my coat pocket. If there was one thing certain to make me scream in fright, it was a mouse. The sight of the creatures with their bulging eyes, twitching whiskers, tiny, scratching paws and teeth that would do Nosferatu proud, have always sent me screaming for the nearest chair. To this day, quite how I managed to hold myself together as he scurried up my arm, I will never understand. I am only thankful that he didn't take the form of a rat.

Torch, and Lucifer, in my pocket I stepped back into the corner. This time the intruder made no effort to hide their progress through the house and, after opening several doors, stepped into the office.

Breath caught in my chest as the intruder shone torchlight around the walls. Light fell on the curtain and the bookshelf, and illuminated the edge of my raincoat but, to my relief, they seemed oblivious to my presence.

I remained still as they began to rifle through the box files, taking box after box from the shelves.

As the noise continued, I took courage and peered from my hiding place. The intruder was dressed from head to foot in black. A black woollen hat hid their hair, and from the bulky dark hoodie they wore, I couldn't determine whether it was male or female. With their back to me, they crouched over the box files, flicking through the paperwork then stacking them neatly on a growing pile before reaching for another one. Whoever it was, was going through each of Selma's boxes in a methodical fashion. This was someone looking for something in particular and determined to find it. I realised then that I would be squashed into the corner for several hours to come.

As we waited, Lucifer's squirming in my pocket made my flesh creep. After this horrifying experience, I wasn't sure I'd be able to look him in the eyes again, never mind let him sit beside me or stroke his glossy fur. As I continued to watch the intruder rifle through the files, I realised that the shock of seeing Lucifer at the door had dissipated the growing heat in my body and stopped the fizzing at my fingers. Which meant, although technically it hadn't been my efforts that had stopped it, the uncontrollable could be controlled, I just had to figure out how.

More than an hour passed and still the intruder searched through the boxes. By now, their calm and orderly efforts had descended into irritated flicking and throwing of checked box files into a pile. The neat stack had fallen at least an hour ago, flinging files into a messy, angular heap across the carpet.

My feet were aching, and my thigh muscles burned with the effort of remaining still. Plus, it was past midnight and it was a struggle to keep my eyes open. The last days had been an emotional roller coaster and I really needed to rest. A low throb started at the back of my head as my eyes burned.

Finally, with every box file gone through, the intruder turned to the desk and, in a final fit of temper, crashed the drawer shut and stamped from the room.

The house filled with the noise of stamping feet and then the crash of pictures being knocked from the wall. Glass shattered. After several minutes, it became obvious that the intruder had left the house.

I stepped out from the gap, every joint in my body complaining and pulled off my coat, dropping it to the floor. Mouse-Lucifer, whiskers bristling, poked his head out of the pocket. I panicked.

"Turn back, turn back, turn back. I need you to be a cat!"

In an instant Lucifer transformed into his usual self, ripping the seams of my pocket as he enlarged. He signalled his outrage with a sharp swish of his tail and stepped out of the torn fabric.

"The power has gone to your head, Livitha Winifred Erikson."

My cheeks burned. "Don't say that name!"

"Hah! Which name is that, dear?" He drawled, a note of spite in his voice. "Winifred?" He rolled the word in his mouth, drawing out the vowels.

"Yes, Winifred. I loathe it."

"I know."

I swear he smirked then, but he sat nonchalantly licking his paw.

"Just stop being mean, Lucifer!"

"Well, stop using your magic on me! I can transform myself more than adequately."

I huffed, but I was not going to bicker with him. "We have to go."

"Indeed, but haven't you forgotten something?"

I picked up my tattered coat.

"No, no! The book." He motioned to the book with the manila file.

"I wonder if that's what they were looking for?"

"You wonder!" He swished his tail and disappeared onto the landing.

I picked up the file, along with some of the original papers I had checked through, and followed Lucifer to the stairs, shining the torch on the mess of broken picture frame and glass now littered on wooden treads.

The picture in the fallen frame was the award Selma had received for 'Outstanding Journalism' from her newspaper. The frame was snapped along one edge, the glass shattered and powdery where the heavy-booted intruder had stood on it, perhaps grinding their heel at its centre.

I replaced the picture on the step and made my way to the kitchen. The door was open, and torchlight shone outside. *You have got to be kidding!* Male voices accompanied the light.

"Hide!" Lucifer hissed as torchlight was trained into the kitchen through the window.

I squatted behind Selma's marble topped kitchen island as two police officers entered the property and bright beams of torchlight illuminated the kitchen. As they walked past the island, I scooted to the other end, circling the cupboard until I was close to the door. Oblivious to me, they made their way into the house and I slipped out into the garden.

"Over here!" Lucifer called. Again, silvery eyes lit by moonlight, peered at me from the darkness.

"I wish you'd stop doing that," I reprimanded as I crouched beside him at the back of Selma's shed.

"Do what?"

"Look at me with those eyes."

"I only have one pair of eyes, Livitha. I can hardly change them."

"Well, can't you at least stop them looking so ... bright?"

It was half an hour before the police officers left and we waited another ten to be sure they had gone from the street. Unable to climb the tree to my own garden, I slipped through the gate, clinging to the shadows, and returned to the car.

Chapter Thirteen

By the time I reached the cottage it was well past the witching hour and a headache nearing a migraine was squeezing my brain in a vice-like grip. Too tired to go through the documentation, or even uncover the secret of the manila envelope, I made my way to bed. I was anxious to go through the material but wanted to do it when I could think clearly, without the overwhelming fog of tiredness.

I slept fitfully, my dreams again filled with fire and unseen entities swarming in the shadows. I watched from above, intuitively feeling their presence. Their collective energies were darkly poisonous, and the shadows pulsed with evil. I woke engulfed by fear and sat up with a jolt as my fingertips sparked. Tiny spirals of smoke rose from the duvet, the fabric glowing orange where sparks had fallen.

"What on earth!" I gasped, leaving the bed, and holding my fingers aloft. The tips fizzed painfully, but the sparking quickly diminished. The trails of smoke from the pure white duvet cover disappeared but it was pockmarked by tiny specks of black. I realised then that if I didn't get my witchy powers under control, they could become a danger to us all.

For once, I hadn't woken sodden with sweat, but I showered as usual, dressed, gathered the papers and file collected from Selma's house, and made my way to the kitchen, unable to shake the sense of dread that had engulfed my dreams and followed me into the waking world. It stalked me as I entered the kitchen, but the scene there helped push it back.

Despite the early hour, Beatrice and Thomasin were already busy packing the tinctures bottled yesterday into cardboard boxes whilst Euphemia wrote labels in a beautiful copperplate script. The kitchen was warm, and glowing wall lamps pushed back the grey morning light. Outside, mist rolled in over the lawns and filled the forest floor, shrouding the ferns and lower trunks. It was the kind of early summer morning where the sun would burn off the mist and the day become hot.

"We're working the early shift," Aunt Euphemia beamed, "so we can focus on you today, lovely girl."

She said this with such joy, that the last tendrils of fear uncurled from around my heart and disappeared. My relief must have shown because Aunt Beatrice asked, "Are you alright, Liv?" All eyes on me, their work momentarily forgotten, they waited for my response.

My answer burst out on breath that had caught in my chest. "I nearly set the bed on fire!"

"I knew it."

"Yes, me too. I could sense it in the house."

"I told you, she's gonna blow."

"I think she already did, Thomasin. We all saw the tree."

"It was incredible."

I waited as usual for the circling banter to finish; they would eventually return their focus to me.

"What happened, Livitha?"

"Well, I had this terrible dream, a nightmare really, and when I woke my fingers were sparking and smoke was rising from the duvet!"

The aunts exchanged glances.

"And what did you see in your dream?"

"This time not much, but I knew there was something in the shadows, something bad, like some dark, black energy. I can't describe it better than that, although one image kept repeating."

"Hmm?"

"It was an iron bracelet."

The aunts exchanged more glances but made no comment.

Aunt Thomasin tapped the papers on the table. "And this, I guess, is the result of your sleuthing?" She said this with a wry smile.

Again, I had forgotten about the files. "Yes! And I'm sure now that Selma was killed by someone with an axe to grind."

"Literally an axe?"

"No, not a literal axe."

"Oh, I only wondered if the murder was ... brutal." Aunt Thomasin's eyes glittered in an unseemly fashion.

"Thomasin, you really are a horror-monger!"

"No, it just makes it all the more intriguing. You know I love a good murder."

"Okay, Miss Marple. Show us what you've got."

"Let's make tea first," Aunt Euphemia suggested. "Then we can all dig in!"

Several minutes later, with cups of tea passed around, the pile of papers and the folder sat centre stage on the table. My aunts interest bordered on excitement, and I hugged the fact that there was a folder taped to the back of the hardback book to myself, waiting for the moment of reveal.

I related the events of the night, how Lucifer had scared me and then how the intruder had startled us both. All three aunts burst into fits of giggles as I recounted how Lucifer had changed into a mouse and scurried up my leg and how I'd got my revenge by changing him back to a cat whilst he was still in the pocket of my coat.

"What I don't understand," interjected Euphemia as each aunt reached for a sheaf of paper, "is quite why the police didn't take any of this as evidence."

"I couldn't see any evidence that they had even looked in the office. It was the first thing I thought of to do."

"It does seem odd."

"I find it very strange, given the number of people who hated the woman, that Livitha should be their prime suspect."

"I think perhaps it has a lot to do with my DNA being all over the house."

"That could be true, but didn't you say that the widow had attacked her, and that Selma had to fight her off."

"So, her DNA could have been all over Selma too!"

"True."

"Well, sisters, I think it stinks," Loveday added from the doorway.

"Don't do that, Loveday! You startled me."

She ignored Beatrice, poured a cup of tea, and joined us at the table.

"How is Raif this morning?"

"A little under the weather."

A collective 'Oh' was accompanied by glances among the sisters, but they quickly returned their attention to the evidence.

"These are the papers that were loose in Selma's office. I took them as I'm guessing it's what she was working on before she died."

Each of us scoured the printed sheets, passing them around the table as we finished. The picture they painted was disturbing. Clearly, Selma had stirred up a hornets' nest of hate among several people.

"People really were very angry with her, weren't they!" Euphemia said as the last sheaf had been read.

"There are some very nasty types out for her blood!"

"Well, I think they got their fill."

"Which one do you think did it?"

"There are several avenues I want to follow, but there's something else!" I placed the book on the table then flipped it over to reveal the taped folder.

Chapter Fourteen

"Ooh!" Aunt Euphemia reached for the book and began pickling at the tape. Beatrice gasped. Thomasin clapped her hands.

Aunt Loveday laughed. "Very dramatic, Livitha. You are obviously having a lot of fun sleuthing."

It was true. I was enjoying myself, despite being the prime suspect in this murder.

"Well, I hope this isn't going to become an addiction, Liv." Aunt Thomasin peeled back another length of tape. "I love a good whodunnit but a murder so close to home really isn't healthy!" She laughed at her own wit.

With all eyes on the book, the tape was peeled off and the manila folder released. It struck me then that perhaps the folder would be empty or contain nothing of interest.

The folder, a single piece of beige card folded in half, sat in the middle of the table.

I opened it to reveal the contents.

"What on earth!"

"Oh, good lord!"

"I can't see! What is it ... Oh!"

"As I live and breathe! What have my eyes just seen?"

Opening the file had revealed a slim stack of photographs. Heat rose in my cheeks as I realised what they were images of, and mortification slipped over me like a scalding cloth as my aunts sat in stunned silence. Loveday quickly closed the file with only the top photograph viewed.

"Loveday!" Aunt Thomasin complained. "It's evidence. We need to see what the other photographs contain."

"I need a moment, darling. To recuperate."

Aunt Beatrice giggled then, and Aunt Euphemia snorted. I sat in mortification, the familiar heat beginning to rise, the image now scorched onto my mind.

The photograph had shown my neighbour, the uptight, church-going, do-gooding facilitator of charity balls, long-serving member of the Parish Council, chair of the Women's Institute, and wife of the town's mayor - who also happened to be the editor at the local newspaper - stark naked, in flagrante delicto, with a woman.

"Mrs. Babcock!" I finally managed to splutter, hysteria rising. "It's my neighbour, Marjorie Babcock."

"The surname doesn't really fit," piped up Aunt Beatrice.

At this I burst into fits of giggles and the kitchen erupted with laughter.

"My eyes!" I laughed. "I will never unsee that!"

As the laughter settled, Aunt Loveday re-opened the file. "Amusing as this is, I think we should see the rest."

Communal assent followed and we leaned forward to gawp at the revealing images.

The photographs were carefully laid out on the table and efforts made to view them with an objective, serious, eye. Snorts and giggles were poorly suppressed. Eventually, Aunt Loveday re-stacked the photographs and closed the file. The remaining photographs had shown Mrs. Babcock in various states of undress with her female lover. It was obvious that the photographs had been taken on a number of occasions. Whoever had taken them had been spying on the poor woman for quite some time.

"Well!" Aunt Loveday said. "I hope never to have to look at those again. And do you know what I think, sisters?"

"Tell us."

"I think these are motive enough for murder."

"But surely you can't think that Mrs. Babcock murdered Selma?" I said. "She's on the Parish Council for goodness sake."

"It's often the quiet ones, Liv," Aunt Thomasin said with a knowing look.

I mulled this over. "The thing is, Mrs. Babcock, Marjorie, is quite a small woman, and whoever was rifling through Selma's office seemed larger."

"Hmm. So, it could be someone else?"

"Yes, it could be. Maybe a man."

"We should hand these over to the police and let them take charge from here."

"But then they'd know I'd broken into the house," I sputtered. "We can't hand them in."

"It could be an anonymous gift."

"I'm not sure I trust them," Aunt Loveday countered. "Why didn't they search the office for evidence? As Livitha said, it is the first thing she thought to do. Any detective worth his salt would surely come to the same conclusion."

"True, but you know it was a Blackwood who came here to question Liv."

A collective hiss.

"Is he the one in charge of the case?"

"He is."

Another sucking of breath.

"What's wrong with it being 'a Blackwood'?" I asked, smarting at their prejudice. That my aunts were holding Garrett Blackwood up for scrutiny and casting him in a negative light caused a physical pain.

"Well, the Blackwoods are cursed, darling," Aunt Loveday explained.

I was left reeling at this information as the conversation continued.

"This whole thing stinks!" Aunt Thomasin interjected. "The evidence is ignored by the police, and then we discover that a Blackwood is in charge of the investigation."

"It does stink."

"Are you suggesting that the evidence was ignored on purpose?"

"Well, it would be gross incompetence otherwise."

"But Garrett was always such a good person," I said remembering the months we spent together.

"He's a Blackwood."

"Yes, you've said, but-"

"I think it's *him*."

The room grew silent, and all eyes locked onto Aunt Loveday.

"Him?" I asked in confusion. "Garrett?"

Ignoring me, Aunt Loveday continued. "As I said, sisters, there is something rotten about the whole situation and the evidence points towards the truth of the matter being obfuscated by *him*. It carries the hallmarks of his work."

"Surely not, Loveday. Not after all this time."

"This is vital evidence, Euphemia. So, why would it be ignored?"

"And there's Livitha's dream to consider."

"How has he found us? We've been so careful." Aunt Euphemia's voice was almost a whisper.

"I don't think the police had even bothered to go into her office," I said, unsure of quite what to say.

"Exactly, which is why I believe that something else is afoot, or rather someone."

"Livitha's dreams could be a warning!"

"Do you really think so? After all these years?"

Once again, I was the observer in a conversation as my aunts discussed the situation. The name 'Old Moleface' was used interchangeably with 'Old Wartface', and on one occasion 'Warty McWartface'. I was relieved. The culprit in their scenario, 'Old Wartface' was not Garrett Blackwood. The conversation went round in circles for several minutes before I said, "Who on earth is Old Moleface?" The room became quiet in an instant and four pairs of sparkling eyes in various shades of blue, violet, green, and turquoise turned to me with a pitying glance.

Not one of the aunts spoke.

"So, who is he?"

"Livitha, there is so much we have to teach you, much of it wondrous and fantastical, but there is a dark history too, that you must understand ... and prepare for."

"Prepare for?" I waited with dread anticipation.

"Tell her, Loveday."

"He, the one I suspect is behind this obfuscation of evidence, and the reason the police are focusing their attention on you, is Matthew Hopkins."

Aunt Beatrice let out a pained groan and the lights in the room flickered.

I stared at Loveday with blank eyes. I had no idea who Matthew Hopkins was. The name meant nothing.

"Matthew Hopkins," she repeated. "The Witchfinder General."

Chapter Fifteen

"A Witchfinder General? But there are no Witchfinder Generals in England. We don't execute witches here anymore."

"No, and that's because we managed to defeat him."

"Loveday put a strong curse on him, but he managed to go underground."

"He faked his own death and no one knows quite what happened, reports say that he died of tuberculosis, others that he was himself executed for witchcraft, but I know this for certain, Matthew Hopkins, Witchfinder General is not the man who is buried beneath the gravestone that carries his name. And you may ask how I know this ..."

I hadn't asked, but I urged her to continue. A broad smile broke across her face. "I know this because I've checked. In his coffin!"

"You dug up a grave?"

"I did."

This information shocked me. Of all the aunts, Loveday was the most genteel and reserved. I couldn't imagine her taking a shovel and digging through the earth, never mind removing the lid of a dead man's casket. Beatrice poked me in the ribs. "She didn't do the digging herself, lovie."

That made sense. I offered an 'Oh' but threw Beatrice a disapproving frown. She gave a shameless shrug of her shoulders in return.

"The body in the casket was Edwin Morland, a young man who had died in the assizes a few days prior. I assume Matthew paid someone to place the body in the coffin."

"We've watched his shenanigans for years. Whenever you hear of a witch being tortured and killed, he's very often behind it."

"Yes, the monster! We've managed to stay safe in our haven."

"Our sanctuary, Haligern cottage. But I fear that your power, Liv, is drawing him close."

"I don't understand. Matthew Hopkins was mortal—he was just a man, so how can he still be alive?"

"Oh, he is far older than you can imagine. The Witchfinder's form took shape as Matthew Hopkins, but he was around for centuries before that, a being of pure evil whispering poison into men's hearts. His fame in that form stuck, and so did the name."

"We were *cunning* folk in my time," Loveday continued. "Men and women who understood natural magic and how to heal the sick and bring positive energy to our people. But Matthew began to whisper his hateful message, an earworm of poison among the superstitious and afraid, and so began the hunts and the burnings."

"He claims to have a book listing every witch in England, alive or dead."

"We've kept him at bay by creating a shield of magic around our home, but I think the strength of your gift has attracted him. It emits its power like a beacon, and his radar has picked it up. People now are more accepting of witches - they won't execute us - so I believe he is manipulating the situation to destroy your life in another way."

I felt faint at that point and took a sip of tea. "But if he knows about me, then he must know about Haligern cottage."

"Don't fret. Our magic is strong. The shield intact. It blinds him to our presence."

"Are you sure?"

"Yes, I'm sure."

"But I could lead him to you, to us!"

"As long as our magic remains intact, the shield will remain. I am more concerned about your safety when you step beyond the boundary of Haligern cottage."

"Sisters, I think we must brace ourselves for more conflict."

The atmosphere in the kitchen had become uncharacteristically heavy and dour, and I instinctively opened the door. A fresh breeze blew into the room and sunlight shone on the flagstones. Beatrice sighed with relief. "That's better! I say we all take a walk to lighten our mood ... and then begin preparations for the Solstice."

Chapter Sixteen

Another day passed and thoughts of Selma and her killer filled my mind. The conclusion that Mrs. Babcock had killed Selma didn't sit well with me, and my thoughts kept returning to the rage-filled and threatening emails, and the files of research I had found in her office. I decided that I had to dig deeper and discover who the emails were from and what Selma was working on at the time of her death.

The lurid photographs gave me an idea, and I placed one in my bedside drawer (face downwards) as an insurance policy. The others I slipped into in my bag, secure within a sealed envelope, then readied myself to leave.

My decision to go back to town was met with resistance, but it was something I felt compelled to do.

"You can't leave, Liv! The Solstice is so close." Aunt Euphemia held an ancient tin pot, with an extremely long and narrow spout, mid-air. Filled with a mixture brewed that morning, she was busy adding a single drop of the liquid to a row of bottles on the table. Bright sunlight glinted on the bottles. Some were of pink glass, others of green, or blue, all looked handmade, and none looked under a hundred years old. Once filled, corks were used as stoppers then melted wax poured over the top as a seal. On the front were newly affixed labels, each written in Aunt Euphemia's beautiful copperplate script. Some had inscriptions in runes, others in an alphabet I struggled to recognise. Several were clearly English though oddly spelled.

"They're for my shop!" Aunt Beatrice beamed as she caught my gaze. "I had hoped that you'd come with me today, Liv. I need some help to tidy round."

"You need a builder and a skip, Beatrice!" Aunt Loveday offered.

Aunt Beatrice only offered a sparkling smile. "Yes! It's so exciting, isn't it."

Aunt Loveday turned back to her own simmering pot with a despairing shake of her head then added some more calendula petals from the garden to the lye mixture. Along with various creams and ointments, the aunts made their own soap from flowers they'd grown and oils they'd pressed. Some they traded with the villagers, and one particular mixture was put by for a family who suffered from what I heard Aunt Beatrice once refer to as 'elfin marks' but which Loveday insisted was a particularly bad case of psoriasis that no modern medicine could touch. A small noise from upstairs caught Aunt Loveday's attention and she removed the pan from the heat and left the kitchen with a sigh.

"I can help when I come back," I offered as Beatrice began to chatter about her shop.

"That will be lovely dear. We need to fill it with energy, and you seem to have a little extra these days."

"I think her energy is a little too erratic at the moment, Beatrice." Euphemia replaced the long-spouted pot on the table. "After the Solstice-"

"She'll be brimming with magic!" Violet eyes shimmered with gold flecks as Aunt Beatrice cast me a glance.

"Exactly!"

"Still, it may be a little too much for the shop."

Unsure of quite how my 'energy' would have any impact on the shop, I steered the conversation back to Selma, and my need to go back to town and uncover the truth about her murder.

Again, my plans were met with resistance with the remaining aunts offering reasons why I shouldn't go.

"We'll be so worried until you return."

"I shall be on tenterhooks until she is back under this roof!" Aunt Thomasin declared. Of the three aunts, she was the only one not busy on the ointment production line. Instead, she sat with a box of cornflowers, sweet nettles, and lavender, and was busy weaving them with grasses and long strings of ivy. Reciting words that I could not understand, her fingers wove the flowers into intricate garlands. She seemed distracted and quickly ignored the chattering in the room to look back out across the lawn.

"Þu miht wiþ attre and wið onflyge

Þu miht wiþ þam laþan ðe geond lond færð"

As she recited the ancient charm the words morphed in my mind, and the unintelligible became understood. As she worked, the magic of the charm was woven into the garland along with the herbs and flowers.

'Your power against poison and against infection

Your power against the loathsome one who travels through the land.'

I marvelled at how clear the meaning was for me now, how I could hear the soft cadence of the ancient language yet understand it too, my brain translating as she spoke. My fingers fizzed, but this time it wasn't anxiety that had kicked it off. With Aunt Thomasin's words repeating as her deft fingers wove together the cornflower, lavender, sweet nettle, and ivy, I continued to answer my aunts concerns with assurances that I wouldn't miss the Solstice.

"I'll be back, I promise."

"What about Old Moleface?"

"Old Moleface?"

"Yes, yes! Old Warty. Matthew Hopkins. Tsk, Livitha! Weren't you listening to us yesterday?

"Yes of course I listened!" I replied. The truth was that I hadn't forgotten about the threat of the Witchfinder General, I had dismissed it. It seemed a step too far to believe that a man would travel through time to hunt us down.

"He's real, Livitha," Aunt Beatrice scolded.

"I know. I'm sorry, it's just with everything else that's going on – being accused of murder and hunted down by the police – he kind of slipped my mind."

"You must take it seriously."

"I will! I am, but I have to find out who killed Selma and clear my name. I'm sure that I'll be safe from Old Wartface, and I can't stay hidden here forever!"

"Oh, Liv. What a mess!"

"I've got an idea that I need to explore," I said. "But I will be back in time for the Solstice. I promise"

"But that's days away! He could track you down and-"

"I'll be fine. Honestly."

Aunt Thomasin placed a handful of flowers she had just begun to weave on the table and gave me her full attention. "Well, if you insist, I have an early gift for you." She rose from the table. "Mind, it won't be as powerful as it should be, and you can only use it once, but here ... just wait a moment."

I waited for several minutes as Aunt Thomasin moved about the kitchen. I waited several more, but still no gift was produced.

"Aunt Thomasin, do you have the gift? I'd really like to leave in the next few minutes. Perhaps I can have it when I get back?"

"Patience, dear girl. I'm feeling my age this morning."

"Which is?" I let the frustration of being kept from beginning my journey, and implementing my plan, get the better of me. Aunt Thomasin graciously ignored my rudeness.

"A lady never divulges that, my dear," she replied with good humour.

"Ask her what she liked best about kissing Thomas Cromwell." Beatrice gave me a wink, in full knowledge that she would be overheard.

"I was naïve, Beatrice. As they say these days, 'Don't judge'! And anyway, I was young, and so was he. It was before he got tangled up with Henry and grew to look so ... pompous. I was only a girl."

Beatrice cackled. I calculated the years and had to bite back my words. I knew that Thomas Cromwell, Henry VIII's chief minister, was born somewhere around 1500 which would make my Aunt Thomasin in the region of five hundred years old if she had been around to kiss the man. "I bet you were very beautiful then, Aunt Thomasin,"

"I was."

"You still are."

"Oh, fiddlesticks!" she said, but I could see by the glitter in her eyes, and the suppressed smile, that she liked my compliment. It was true, she was still beautiful. "At least I was until I took this form. I only wish I could have taken a slightly younger age, but Loveday-"

"Shh, Thomasin! She'll hear you and I couldn't bear that."

I looked at my aunts with curiosity. Living with them now was like peeling an onion, there were layer after layer of secrets. "Couldn't bear what, Aunt Bee?" I asked, determined to discover what lay beneath this particular layer.

"Well," she checked through the open door. "It's for her that we look as we do."

"Elegant and beautiful?"

"No, silly. Old."

"But you've always looked old, I mean ... this way."

"We could have looked much younger."

"Oh," I said, my curiosity spiralling. "So, why do you look ... like this?"

"So that Raif doesn't get upset."

"Or Loveday."

"Yes, or Loveday. It would hurt her terribly if she thought Raif was unhappy."

"I'm completely confused now. What has you looking ... old, got to do with Raif or Aunt Loveday being unhappy?"

"He doesn't age as we do."

"But he looks the same as you do."

"Exactly!"

"Exactly what?"

"He's mortal, dear. The only reason he is still with us is because of Loveday's magic. But he still ages, although very, very slowly."

"Very slowly! When Loveday met him, he was the spitting image of the portrait on the gallery landing."

"Psht! Beatrice, that *is* a painting of Raif. Loveday had it commissioned by the same artist who painted Thomas Cromwell when he worked for Henry."

"Oh, yes! Now, what was his name?"

"It was Hans Holbein the Younger," Aunt Thomasin filled in. "Such a talented artist, and a nice man too."

"I can't remember everything, Thomasin," Beatrice scolded huffily "There are a lot of years stored up here," she tapped a finger at her temple, "and sometimes the old retrieval system is a little glitchy."

"Hark at you with your modern talk!" Thomasin laughed.

"Well, I do like to keep up with the times ... on occasion."

This made me smile. Aunt Beatrice was anything but 'modern'.

"So," Thomasin continued. "When it became obvious that Raif was ageing, despite Loveday's magic, we made a pact to age with him."

I was staggered. The sacrifice my aunts had made, were still making, was enormous.

"He's her soulmate, Liv," Aunt Beatrice explained. "And when you find your soulmate, you don't let go."

It was hard to think much better of my aunts, but I held them in renewed awe. Their selflessness and sisterhood were incredible.

"Anyway, we digress. Back to the gift." Thomasin reached for a leather-bound book on the shelf, leafed through its stiff vellum pages and began to recite in words I couldn't understand. When I imagined my aunts casting a spell, it was always in Latin, but the words Thomasin recited bore no resemblance to that language.

As before, as I continued to listen to her incantation, the words became clear:

"Feond, feond, ferhþgeníðla.

Scring þu alswa scerne awage.

Her ne scealt þu timbrien, ne nenne tun habben,

Napiht geþurþe.

...

Shrivel like dung.

Shrink as the coal upon the hearth!

Become as nought.

Shrivel like dung.

May you become as little as a linseed grain.

And much smaller, likewise, than an earwig's hipbone!

And even so small may you become, that you become as nought.

Shrivel like dung.

Become as nought!

As she spoke, she unwrapped a silver pendant in the shape of a hammer from a fold of soft leather. Reaching for a glass jar she shook out a sprinkle of betony and stuffed the dried herb into the pendant's hollows. She finished with, "Who so betony on him here, from wicked spirits it will him were."

Taking the pendant, she placed it over my head. "There! That should help. Now, remember, if you get into trouble just recite the words 'May you shrink away like dung!'

"Are you serious? Dung?"

"Yes, Livitha, and if you can manage it in our language, then all the better. Remember 'Scring þu alswa scerne awage'. May you shrink away like dung.

"And say it with feeling, Livitha," Aunt Beatrice added then repeated the phrase for emphasis. "Scring þu alswa scerne awage"

"Got it," I confirmed. "May you shrink away like dung. Scring þu alswa scerne awage." The words were unfamiliar on my tongue, but oddly satisfying. And, with the incantation repeating in my mind, I left the cottage.

Chapter Seventeen

Halfway to town, I realised that a car was following me. It had all the classic signs of being an unmarked police car. It increased its speed and slowed when I did and took the same turns. When I pulled over into a passing place, it passed, but was waiting for me further along the road, tucked into a roadside track. Heart pounding, I continued to watch as it followed. A man was driving. He was alone, but the shadows were too dark to allow me to see his face.

In an effort to lose him, I turned off the main road and into a nearby village. He followed, although at a distance, and at one point I thought I'd lost him but as we approached the town, I caught sight of the car once more. Certain that I was under police surveillance, I pulled down a narrow street, quickly took a right, then a left, and pulled into the familiar carpark of our local pub. One parking space was hidden behind some shrubs, an overflow slot that only locals were familiar with, and I pulled my car in and then made my way on foot to the side of the building.

After several minutes without sight of the car, sure that I had now lost whoever had followed me, I made my way to the street and stepped out onto the path.

"Liv!" The voice was instantly familiar; the police officer who had visited the cottage—Garrett Blackwood. "Livitha Erikson!"

Breath caught in my chest.

The need to run was intense, but I turned to face Garrett. His closeness took me by surprise, and I took a step back. He towered above me, so close that I could smell his cologne. Do you know that part in trashy romances where the heroine quivers? I think I 'quivered' as he stood before me, six-foot four of tanned and muscular male smiling down at me as though he had just found a lost treasure.

"Liv!" He said, breathless. "I thought I'd lost you."

I thought I'd lost you at the crossroads! My heart hammered. "No, I'm here," was my pathetic reply. Uncomfortable under his gaze as he searched my face, I regretted every extra slice of cake I had ever eaten, and every afternoon spent in the garden without factor 50 and a wide-brimmed hat to protect my skin.

"Liv!" he repeated.

"Garrett," I smiled.

"So ... this is going to sound strange ..."

I waited for him to continue.

"No matter," he laughed as though uncertain. It was almost as though his confidence was a little shaky, but I dismissed the notion; no one as good looking as Garrett Blackwood could feel that way.

I brushed fingers through my hair, wishing I'd taken just a little longer to style it that morning, or rather made an effort to style it.

"Ignore me. Listen. I do need to talk to you."

I feigned ignorance. "Oh?"

"Yes, you know, about Selma Maybrook."

I nearly asked 'Who?' but that would be a step too far. Instead, still panicking I blurted, "I'm sorry, but I'm kind of busy ... maybe I can meet you at the police station ... later?"

He threw me a bemused glance. "I have a better idea. Why don't we talk now? Join me for a coffee." I was unsure if I had any choice in the matter so agreed.

Ten minutes later, I sat opposite Garrett, intensely aware of his presence, unsure whether he was interested in my conversation or doing his job and watching for nuances of deceit. My imagination was on overload; he would ask me a question that framed me, cry 'Gotcha!', cuff me, then watch with satisfaction as I was bundled into a Black Mariah, another perp captured, just another day at the office for Garrett Blackwood, detective extraordinaire! I made an effort to switch off the rambling and hyperbolic voiceover narrating my downfall, and took a sip of coffee, desperately hoping that no stray hairs had decided to ambush my chin, or top lip, that morning, realising I hadn't checked before I left the house! Coffee cup nearly permanently at my chin as we spoke, I squirmed in my awkwardness.

So far, I had managed to sit opposite Garrett and hold my nerve despite my heart pounding. However, anxiety was fanning the embers of heat at my core and panic was only just beneath the surface. *Stay calm, Liv! You are a strong and confident woman. Sure, but I'm also a nervous wreck, sitting in front of a man who makes my knees weak, and my heart palpitate, and who looks like he belongs on screen playing a superhero rather than sitting opposite a frumpy, middle-aged housewife/murder suspect.* I attempted a smile. I'm sure it emerged as a grimace.

As my fingers began to fizz, my mind scrambled for a distraction, some way of calming myself down.

And then I did something very stupid. "I have something to show you." Slipping a hand into my bag, I withdrew the photographs, fanning them out like cards. "Take one!" I urged with a smile as though attempting a card trick.

He reached for a card, but catching a glimpse of Mrs. Babcock's naked posterior, his face drained of colour and he withdrew his hand as though scorched. "Liv! I ... I'm not into that kind of thing."

A flush rose on my cheeks so intense it seeped into my hairline. I was mortified, horrified that he had, for even one second, assumed I had shown him the photographs for some perverse pleasure. "Take me down now!" I muttered, wanting the ground to swallow me up, then quickly reversed my thinking. Given the state of my nerves, there was no telling in what direction my witchy powers would start misfiring. "No!" *Stay calm!* "No, this is evidence. I can't believe ... Oh my goodness! I am so embarrassed."

"Oh!" He made an effort to laugh, failed, then cleared his throat and said, "Evidence. Then let me see."

I handed him the photographs. "We think that they may be a motive for Selma's murder, but I'm not convinced. All I do know is that it wasn't me."

He flicked through the photographs with professional gravity, unlike the embarrassed hilarity of my aunts.

"We?"

"Yes, my aunts have seen them too"

His brows lifted in surprise. "And where did you acquire this 'evidence'?" He asked, slipping back into detective mode.

It was my turn to cough. Unsure whether I should admit to breaking and entering a crime scene, I tried to fob him off with, "A house."

He eyed me with an expectant raise of his brows. "A house? Which house?"

"On Weland Avenue."

"Liv! Just tell the truth."

"Oh, but you'll arrest me or something! It was a silly thing to do, but I was desperate. Please understand that. When Pascal called me and said I was – I lowered my head and whispered – wanted for murder, I panicked. I knew it wasn't me, so I had to prove it."

"Liv ... what did you do?"

"I went to Selma's house. They were in her desk drawer."

"So, breaking and entering *and* contaminating a crime scene?"

"Well, my DNA was already all over the place!" I said in my defence. "Don't arrest me, please!"

He shook his head in non-committal disapproval, and I eyed the door, ready to bolt.

"You should hand these into the station," he said handing the deck of lurid photographs back to me.

"I can't! They'll arrest me and put me in the cells."

"But I've seen them now Liv, and this – he gestured a hand between us – is a conflict of interests. If I don't report them ..."

"Then just forget about them! Pretend we haven't had this conversation."

He held my gaze then and, for the first time, I made a deliberate effort to use my powers. "Forget, forget, forget, that ever we did meet. I'll put the cards into my bag, and you shall rise to your feet!" He continued to stare at me and then his eyes took on a vacant stare that I assumed was the spell doing its job. I admit it was a pretty awful spell, but it rhymed and seemed to be working.

He glanced around the café, threw me a confused frown, then left. Unable to believe that the spell had worked, and so quickly, I stared after Garrett's disappearing figure. "Forget that ever we did meet", I whispered, realising the import of my words. Pain gripped my heart then, a dull and sorrowful ache that grew more intense the further away Garrett walked.

I paid the bill with gloom descending over me like a wet flannel and made my way to the small hotel where I planned to stay for the next two nights.

Chapter Eighteen

The car had to be collected from the hidden space in the pub's carpark and, as I made my way there, the sensation of being watched became intense. Efforts to shrug it off failed, and the morning took another peculiar turn as I walked across the town's bridge and back towards the pub. The water beneath was slow-flowing and narrow, cleaving this side of town from the other as it eased its way to a wider river. Only one other person was walking on the bridge, a woman, shopping bag already filled with fresh produce from the fruit and vegetable shop in the precinct behind us. The frilled greenery of carrot tops and celery poked out from her eco-friendly canvas shopper. Two men approached from the other side, one seemed nonchalant in blue jeans and leather jacket, the other walked with a hurried intensity. Both seemed to have their focus trained on me but I put this down to paranoia and shifted my gaze to the murky river and the massive brick building that dominated the bank, a leftover from an industrial phase in the town, an old bicycle factory now converted into trendy apartments.

From behind came a sharp tack, tack, tack on the pavement. A quick check showed it to be a black dog, the tack, tack, the noise of its claws on the tarmac. The dog was of medium size with a long and glossy coat, the breed not dissimilar in shape to a border Collie, although I had never seen one with such a dark coat before. Stray dogs were an unusual sight in the town, and with no evidence of a collar, and no sign of an owner, I increased my pace.

In the next moment, the dog sprang into action. It bounded forward with hackles raised and teeth bared, its gaze focused on me. It made no sound and was almost immediately in front of me. Hands held out in defence, I took a step back and came up against a barrier that ruined any chance of escape. The man behind me yelped as I stood on his foot, and I squealed as the dog bounded forward. Fear rippled through me but instead of sinking its teeth into my throat, the dog shot past, sprinting towards another target. Heart pounding, I gasped for breath, stumbling as I attempted to untangle myself from the man I had walked into. His arms circled my waist, a massive bunch of flowers held at my middle, and we teetered forward, locked together as my feet rested on his. Despite my efforts, I remained in the stranger's embrace, uncomfortably aware of his grip around my generous middle. On the other side of the bridge, the dog had found another walker to harass.

In the seconds that followed, he released me, and I leant up against the iron barriers for support. The man towered above me and watched my every reaction. His smile was huge and completely inappropriate for the drama that had just unfolded.

"Sorry!" I said, catching my breath, my heart pounding as adrenaline coursed through my veins. "I didn't mean to crush your feet. The dog-"

"No need to apologise, Liv. You can crush my feet any day of the week. Not ... not that I'm saying you did crush them!" He floundered. "You're not fat enough for that ... I mean ... you're voluptuous, not ... not fat!"

I held a hand up for him to stop and smiled as an offering of peace. His awkwardness was kind of endearing, even if he was reminding me that I was no sylph. I knew I had a few pounds to lose, more than a few, but that wasn't his fault.

"You know me?" I asked picking up on his use of my name.

"Of course!" He said this as though it were the most natural thing in the world that he should. I had no idea who he was.

"Liv!" he said, thrusting the bunch of flowers at me. "These are for you." Pink freesias and cream roses hovered only inches from my face.

Completely taken by surprise, and paralysed by confusion, I could only listen as the man began to speak with the flowers held as an offering between us. In the foreground the black dog had run up to the man in the leather jacket. Thankfully, it hadn't attacked but now trotted by the man's side in semi-menacing fashion. The man waved a hand at the dog to fend it off, but the faster he walked, the quicker the dog trotted at his side. They passed me as I took the flowers and I was left facing the strange man.

"It's me!" the stranger said. "James Belton! You remember me, Liv. We went to school together."

"School?"

"Yes!" For a moment he looked crestfallen, but quickly recovered and continued to offer reminders of our joint history.

My memory began to recall James as a gangling teenage boy in school uniform. He wasn't part of the gang I used to knock about with at breaktimes, so my memories were sparse.

The dog yapped and the harassed man shouted, "Be off with you!" in a gruff voice.

"James Belton!" I exclaimed as though all had become clear. "Of course! I remember you now. How are you?"

"I hope you like the flowers." He gestured to the mixed bunch now gripped in my hand.

"They're gorgeous." It was true, the flowers were stunning and contained some of my favourite blooms. "But I'm not sure why you're giving them to *me*."

"Well, I saw you earlier in the coffee shop and I ... well, I was just overcome with the need to talk to you. You're so beautiful, Liv. I've never forgotten you, you know."

My cheeks began to prickle. Already on edge, James' bizarre attention was tipping me over. I began to flounder. I had never received male attention like this, and it was unnerving. Behind me the dog barked, and his victim yelped. Despite the intense gaze James had me locked in, I turned to the scene. The dog stood at the point where the bridge joined the land, and the man in the leather jacket was running through the precinct. As he darted down one of the cobbled side streets the dog turned to face the bridge once more. It crossed my mind that perhaps the dog was Lucifer in another form, following me again and causing mayhem. The feline did have a wicked streak, and I suspected he was also the bat that had enjoyed tormenting me the night of my fiftieth birthday party.

James continued to smile with a lopsided and expectant grin. Several minutes passed as he complimented me on how beautiful I was, and how wonderful it was that he had seen me at the café that morning. "It's serendipity, Liv. Some call it Fate. I've sometimes spotted you at the supermarket, or shopping in town. I've watched you from afar, Liv.

Great! My own personal stalker. On top of feeling uneasy, I wondered whether being wanted by the police had thrown me into infamy, but James made no mention of Selma.

He continued to babble as I grasped for an appropriate response. "It was mostly Tescos I saw you in, but every now and then you'd be in Lidl's. I like to shop for the best bargains too!" He was rambling and there were moments when he seemed to lose track of his words, then come back to himself. "I've wanted to talk to you for a long time, but of course you were married, but now I know that you're free again, well ... after seeing you this morning, I had to talk to you. It was all I could think of."

Taken aback by the reference to the disintegration of my marriage to Pascal, I offered a pathetic, "I ... er ... thank you," then scrabbled to think of some way of ending the conversation without being impolite.

"I want to take you to dinner!" he blurted. "Tonight."

He said this with such determination that I almost agreed until the black dog trotted past me and broke the spell, giving me crucial seconds to recover. "Well, I'm kind of busy tonight, James. I appreciate the invite but-"

Undaunted, he said, "Tomorrow night then, or lunch tomorrow. Whenever you say, Liv. It's up to you. I'm not letting you slip away this time though!"

He said this with such relish that I took a step back. There was something maniacal about the way his eyes glittered. He seemed obsessed. I felt ridiculous; *how could anyone be interested in a middle-aged frump like me?* "Okay," I placated, unsure of quite how a rejection of his offer would be taken. "How about you give me your number and I'll call you?" I said this without any intention of calling the man, sure now that he was unhinged.

"Yes!" he said. "That's a great idea."

I took my phone out to fake entering his number, but he snatched the mobile from my hand and replaced it with his own. "Let's swap numbers," he said punching in the digits.

Ambushed, I punched in my number and returned the phone.

"Great!" he said with a smile checking the details I had entered. "I'll call you later. I know the perfect place for a romantic dinner for two, just us."

"Sure," I replied with less enthusiasm although I did raise a smile. It was an odd experience, but he seemed to genuinely like me and I was flattered despite the weirdness of his attention.

"See you soon!" he beamed.

"Bye!" I said and waved the flowers at him. "And thanks for these."

He didn't move, and I had to side-step him to continue over the bridge and onwards to collect my car.

There was no sign of the dog.

Chapter Nineteen

My room at the hotel was comfortable and now filled with the heady scent of freesias and tea roses placed in a cut glass vase supplied by the owner. The flowers stood at the centre of a small table set beside a window that overlooked the hotel's courtyard garden. Still bemused, but increasingly flattered by James' offer of dinner, I found myself considering his invitation. I teetered between a flat-out refusal and going along out of curiosity but, berating myself for even thinking of going, and alone in the room, my thoughts returned to Pascal and our home. Displaced and lonely, I missed that feeling of ease, of being able to wander through my house, each room a comfort. My mood began to lower and the emotions that were so often just beneath my veneer of barely managed calm began to bubble. A tear slipped down my cheek.

The mobile rang beside me. Startled, I wiped the tears away and turned it over with apprehension. Heart pounding, the relief was immediate. 'Heligern' was printed on the screen. I answered it immediately, forcing my voice to sound buoyant. Several minutes of polite conversation followed and many questions about my health and progress.

"I only left this morning," I said. "I haven't had time-"

"So, you haven't done any sleuthing?"

I laughed at this quaint phrase. "No, Aunt B. I haven't done any sleuthing."

"So, nothing unusual has happened?"

Not unless showing Garrett Blackwood a stack of pornographic photographs counts! I didn't want to cause unnecessary worry so said, "No, nothing unusual. I've just got to the hotel. I was about to start looking through the files and photos again."

"Garrett Blackwood ... you haven't seen him, then?"

I couldn't lie. "Well, yes. How did you know?"

"I didn't. You did. Does he suspect you?"

"I don't know, but he won't be a problem any longer."

"Aah! So, you're using your powers then."

"Well, kind of."

"He's a Blackwood, Liv. Cursed."

"I know, you've told me. Listen-"

"I will. Now," she said ignoring my efforts to speak, "the important thing, Livitha is to keep your counsel and remember 'dung'!"

Her conversation was becoming disjointed, but before I could question quite what she meant, the phoneline went dead. Talking on the telephone with my aunts had always been awkward, none seemed to enjoy using the technology, all holding it with varying degrees of suspicion.

"Bye to you too," I laughed as I set the phone back down. "Keep my counsel and remember dung!"

Bumped out of my morose state, I made a cup of coffee and decided to spend the next hour or two scouring the files and photographs in the hope that they would offer some clue, or trigger my thinking down a useful avenue.

I returned to the printed emails, re-reading the threats, some of them quite graphic, and wondered how Selma had coped with the level of abuse thrown at her. It became obvious, as I pieced the information together, that there were two threads running through. One seemed to be a response to blackmail, or some threat offered by Selma herself. The other pertained to a case she was working on. It was obvious that both parties regarded Selma as a threat and I began to wonder quite how far this ruthless woman would go, or to what level she would stoop, to get her story.

The photographs offered nothing new until I looked beyond the women's naked flesh and took note of the backgrounds. They appeared to have been taken in two locations, one was a bedroom whilst the other was an office, the images captured by hidden cameras. The bedroom was nondescript with only an ornate mirror caught in one corner of the room. The office was sparsely equipped with a clock on the wall, a desk and chair. The only other item in the office appeared to be a stack of papers on top of a filing cabinet. All other items were obscured by the women's fleshy bodies.

Several of the emails threatened legal action. One from the same organisation made more personal threats. I decided to focus on discovering just who had sent them and where they worked. I would need to track down Selma's colleague and discover exactly what project she was working on. To do that I would need Mrs. Babcock's help. I left the hotel with a clear sense of mission.

With the car parked several streets away from my house, I entered Weland Avenue on foot and was surprised to see the black dog standing beside the road sign. It had to be Lucifer, there was no other explanation. The dog stood its ground as I approached, and only when I grew close did it seem to become wary.

With only three feet between us, I asked, "So, what exactly are you doing here? I told you to stay at home!"

The dog looked at me with quizzical eyes. There was nothing familiar about them.

I tried again, unsure now. "Is that you, Lucifer?" I cast a quick glance around. Anyone who saw me talking to the dog, and waiting for a reply, would think me more than a little strange. The dog merely cocked its head to one side and threw me a confused look. If it was Lucifer, he was doing a good job of keeping up the pretence. I held the dog's gaze for a few more seconds then dismissed the idea. There was no hint that the dog was in fact Lucifer: no dismissive swishing of the tail, and no disapproving looks. With another quick glance around, and re-assured that I hadn't been seen, I walked onwards to my house.

To my relief, Pascal wasn't home, and I let myself in.

Although I had only been with my aunts for a few days, re-entering the house already felt uncomfortable. Something inside it had shifted, and the energy felt wrong. I walked through the house opening curtains and windows, allowing the light and fresh air to breathe through it once more. Despite the light now flooding the rooms, the house remained oppressive. It was a feeling I had never encountered there before. My beautiful house had always been a sanctuary, its light refreshing, and its energy mellow and welcoming.

In an effort to rid myself of the unease, I put on the kettle then flung the backdoor open, stepping out into the sunlight and breathing in the fresh air as though I had just resurfaced from a very deep and watery dive. My vision clouded for a moment and then everything shimmered with iridescent blues and greens. Steadying myself for a few moments, I waited until my vision cleared. Nothing seemed amiss - I hadn't had a stroke or some other bodily malfunction - and I dismissed the vision as a trick of the light then walked through my garden, noting each new bloom that had arrived, thanking it silently for the joy and beauty it brought.

As I made my way around, I noticed a change. A gap had appeared in the hedge, giving a clear view of Mr. Grayson's garden. "Nosey old sod!" I muttered and strode down to the hedge to inspect the damage. There was no evidence of clipping or lopping, instead the shrub was dying, its leaves brown, crisp and curling, and they crumbled in my hand. Beside the bush, the roses I had planted last year were also showing signs of struggle, and their leaves were marked with black spots, their buds dying on the stem. I knew that for all his faults Mr. Grayson loved the natural world and took great joy from his own garden. I couldn't imagine him sabotaging mine. As I walked back through the garden, I noticed other signs of damage – broken stems and petals strewn about the grass. I presumed they had fallen from dying heads but on closer inspection could see they had been deliberately pulled off and strewn across the grass. My precious flowers had been vandalized! Was it Pascal's doing? Did he hate me that much? Did he really believe I murdered Selma?

As I struggled with my thoughts, the night drew in, casting a twilight glow across the garden and shadows began to creep over the lawn. The house looked back at me with blank eyes and for the first time I didn't want to step back inside.

Crunching gravel in the driveway announced Pascal's arrival home and, as I began to panic, a light flickered in Selma's office window. It could be the intruder from yesterday and I determined to find out.

Once again, I climbed the tree and slipped into Selma's garden. As I reached her kitchen door Pascal shouted 'Hello!' and I remembered that I had left my bag on the kitchen table. It was too late to retrieve it now; I would face Pascal's questioning later *and* confront him about the garden! Right now, I had to discover just who was in Selma's house.

Chapter Twenty

Selma's immaculate kitchen resembled a bomb site. Dirty footprints now tracked across her once gleaming white tiles and the contents of several cupboards lay strewn across the floor and worktops. The distinctive noise of someone opening drawers and then sliding her full-length and mirrored wardrobe doors open came from upstairs. Selma's house was being ransacked. I faltered then, my bravado slipping; it could be a bona fide burglar, someone armed and dangerous. Hovering at the open kitchen door, one foot on the flagstones outside, I listened. Whoever was upstairs was working their way through the house, moving from bedroom to bedroom.

As the noise continued, Pascal stepped into our garden, and called my name. The hedge hid Selma's garden from view, but I slipped back inside the house just in case. From upstairs came a crash as something was knocked to the floor. It was followed by a curse and then, 'Where the very heck did you hide them?' A growl of frustration that rose to a squeal followed. The voice was a woman's! I took courage from that; a woman was far less threatening than a man, at least I thought so at the time. Various items had been removed from the drawers, and I took a rolling pin, surprised that Selma even had one.

Rolling pin firmly in hand, I made my way to the stairs. The fallen picture frame lay between risers surrounded by glass. I stepped around it, resisting the urge to re-hang it, and made my way to the landing. The noise of drawers and cupboards being opened, and their contents rifled, continued. In my mind's eye I saw the woman. Dressed all in black, a balaclava pulled down over her face, her eyes and mouth were bright hollows against the fabric as she maniacally searched through Selma's belongings. As I stepped up to the office door, the scavenger grunted, and another drawer opened with a clat. I took another step closer. Torchlight wavered in the room.

I pushed the door a little more ajar and peered in.

The woman was exactly as I had imagined, or almost! Dressed all in black, her hair was tucked into a black beanie pulled low over her brows. She wore a black raincoat tightly belted at the waist with the collar pulled up. The beanie was out of place, but the raincoat was familiar as was the woman it covered. I recognised her immediately—Marjorie Babcock!

Unaware of my presence, she continued to rifle through Selma's drawers. Pulling the bottom drawer open, the one where I had discovered the hidden manila envelope and its reputation-destroying photographs, she rifled through the remaining papers then slammed it shut, stifling a sob. Sniffling, she wiped tears away with her sleeve. My heart went out to her then. "Marjorie!" I called from the doorway. She jumped like a startled rabbit and shone the torchlight directly into my eyes. I was unprepared for what happened next.

Blinded, I shielded my eyes and in the next moment was thrust against the doorframe as Marjorie charged. Her speed and agility were a huge surprise, she must have taken a great bound across the office to reach me in such short time.

Pain rang through the back of my skull as my head knocked against the frame and my breath left me as she barged into me, elbow jabbing into my abdomen. The doorframe was narrow, or perhaps I was a little wide, and Marjorie's efforts at a quick getaway failed. She stumbled over my feet, landing with a thud and a heavy grunt on the carpet. "Marjorie! Wait!" I said as she scrabbled against me without consideration to the pain she was causing. Knees and boots knocked into my shins and calves and I yelped in pain as she pulled and kicked her way to a standing position. The rolling pin dropped from my hands. She made no effort to speak and with a final huge push forced me into the office and sprinted to the top of the landing.

"Marjorie! Wait!"

Glass crunched beneath her feet as she ran down the stairs. A clat as she made contact with the picture frame was followed by a curse and then a squeal as she lost her footing. A series of thuds followed.

By the time I made it to the landing, she was attempting to stand, one hand clinging to the bannister. "Marjorie! I know what you're looking for."

She froze then, half standing, and stared at me. I reached a hand to my bag – the bag I normally wore across my shoulder – and remembered it was on the table at home. She took a step back as though afraid. "Marjorie, it's me, Liv Carlton, from next door."

"I know who you are. You murdered Selma!"

"No!" I gasped. "Of course I didn't."

"Bill Grayson said he heard you threaten to kill her."

"No, not threaten to kill her. I said I wished she were dead." It seemed ludicrous that I had just caught Marjorie burgling her dead neighbour's house, yet I was the one having to defend myself. "She was having an affair with Pascal!" Marjorie only grunted at this. "And when Bill Grayson heard me, I'd just caught them at it! In my beautiful garden." The pain of the moment came back to me then, but I swallowed down the emotion.

"Well, I suppose I'd be upset too if that happened to me."

I took tentative steps towards her, the rolling pin firmly in my hand. Given her extreme reaction upstairs, I didn't trust her not to knock me out and call the police. The torchlight blinded me once more. "I can't see to come down, Marjorie."

"Well, maybe it's safer if you stay there." There was an edge in her voice.

"Hey, I'm not the one ransacking Selma's house! And I didn't kill her. Put the torch down, there's something we need to talk about."

In the kitchen, moonlight was sufficient to light the room to grey and I convinced Marjorie to switch off the torch. Alerting more neighbours to our presence was the last thing I wanted-ed.

"I have a proposition for you."

"Oh?"

"Yes. I know for one hundred percent sure that I didn't kill Selma, but I want to find out who did."

"Have you any idea who did it?"

"I've got my suspicions."

"Well ... who?"

I stalled then, not wanting to share the details, but I needed Marjorie's co-operation for the next part of my plan. "I think it was one of her colleagues. Someone jealous of her success. On the night she came back from the funeral, she was angry and called one a 'backstabbing pig'". The part about the colleague was true, but not the real reason I needed Marjorie's help.

"And just how am I supposed to help with that?"

"Well, I want to talk to her colleagues – without them knowing – I want you to get me a job in the office."

"Hah! What is it about that newspaper!" She huffed. "I don't see why you can't just talk to her colleagues. Tell them you're doing an investigative piece on her death." She shrugged her shoulders.

"And alert them? One of them may be the killer!"

"You should just leave it to the police. DCI Blackwood is the man you should talk to, he's very reasonable."

"The police have me down as the prime suspect and I know I'm innocent. If I turn myself in, then I'll never get the chance to prove my innocence. Anyway, they're so far off the mark, I just don't trust them to get it right."

She turned then and I knew I had to put pressure on her. "Marjorie, I need your help."

"I'm sorry, but it's not something-"

"I have the photos."

I let the sentence hang between us. She turned back on her heels, her eyes now boring into mine.

"Where are they?"

"At my house. Pascal has them," I lied.

Unsteady, she grasped the bannister.

"But he hasn't seen them. I'm the only one who has." I lied again, just a white lie to protect her; there was no need to offer up the vision of a snickering group of elderly women - women I knew she admired - pointing at her bare bottom. "I'm guessing that's what all this is about." I gestured to the mess in the kitchen. She nodded. The kitchen and Marjorie were greyed out in the moonlight but I'm sure her cheeks were a shade of puce.

"Can I have them ... please?"

"If you can help me."

She nodded again.

"Thank you!" I took the remaining steps down the stairs. The moment was awkward. "I ... the woman in the photos ... she's very pretty."

Marjorie let out an odd mewl and simply nodded.

"Yes," she managed. "She is. We're in love you know. It's nothing sordid. I'd marry her if I could but ... Frank would cut me off – you have no idea of who he knows – and ... and my reputation would be shot!"

I thought about the charity balls she hosted, and the country fetes etcetera.

"I understand Marjorie."

"I do love her!" This admission was followed by a sob, and I placed a comforting arm around her shoulder. "Selma was a beast taking those photographs."

"Was she blackmailing you?"

A vociferous nod was accompanied by a sniff. "Yes! When she died, I knew I had to find the photos before someone else did."

"There, there," I soothed. "I have them so there's nothing to worry about."

"Huh!" she huffed, rounding on me. "Apart from the fact that now you're blackmailing me too!"

"No!" I said, not wanting that accusation piling on my head along with murder. "I just need your help. You can have the photographs back."

"Can I?"

"Yes, of course. I'll get them now."

"You will?" she asked this as though a child.

"Yes. I'll bring them across to your house."

She agreed to this and seemed relieved as we walked to the front of the house, both hugging the shadows. All I had to do now was collect my bag from the kitchen, avoiding Pascal if possible.

Chapter Twenty-One

I watched Mrs. Babcock cross the road then returned to my own house. Opening the front door with stealth, I tiptoed down the hall. I had expected to hear evidence of Pascal in the shower – he liked to shower after returning from work – or preparing dinner in the kitchen, but the house was quiet, and that same oppressive energy I had sensed earlier still hovered within its walls. It wasn't until I reached the door leading from the hallway into the kitchen that I heard the noise. Pascal was laughing, or rather attempting to subdue hysterical laughter. The snort would erupt then grow quiet, then erupt again and be followed by wheezing laughter.

Another step forward and I was at the kitchen threshold. Pascal stood with his back to me, his shoulders heaving, wiping tears from his face with his shirt sleeve. The contents of my bag were spilled out across the table and in his hands were Marjorie's photographs. He snorted and spluttered with each new image.

"Having fun, Pascal?"

He spun to me, all mirth gone, then immediately burst into hysterical laughter. I couldn't help a smile. Only embarrassment as my aunts had looked through the images prevented me laughing too.

"So, Liv, the wind's blowing in a new direction, eh?"

"What? No!" Mortification slid over me once more as I understood the gist of Pascal's words. "No! I found them."

"Found them?"

"Yes!"

"Where on earth did you find porn ... photographs of Mrs. B? Does she do it ... professionally?"

"Oh, my goodness, Pascal! No, of course not."

"Then enlighten me. Tell me why my wife has pornographic photographs – and a good number too – of our holier-than-thou neighbour."

I realised then that I'd have to admit to breaking into Selma's house. "They were in Selma's desk. She took the photographs, and she's been blackmailing Marjorie."

All hilarity gone Pascal sat down at the table with a thud. The next hour was spent explaining everything I had discovered about Selma and Marjorie, and my plans. It took some time before he would believe me or take me seriously. I found this irksome, but needed his help, so just smiled at his derisory comments, and began to wonder what I'd ever seen in him.

Holding his hands up as though in surrender, he said, "Alright, Liv. I believe you. I never really believed you killed Selma, but the detective who came was so adamant that you had."

"Adamant? Don't you find it strange that they should be so certain it was me? It seems odd that a detective would tell you that just a day after her death. Did they even have time to get the test results back?"

"I have no idea, Liv. I know nothing about police procedure."

"Me neither, only what I've seen on the telly." I mulled this over for a moment. "What did he look like, this detective?"

"Well ... he was tall. I'd say a little younger than me. Dark hair but greying at the sides. And he was with a rather voluptuous blonde. Nice looker too!"

I ignored the comment about the blonde, appalled that I had ignored similar comments hundreds of times over the past twenty-six years, and pushed him to describe the male officer. "Any distinguishing marks?"

He laughed. "You're already beginning to sound like a copper. I'd best watch my speed the next time we're out."

His presumption that we'd ever take a ride out together was annoying, as was his derisive comment about my questioning, but again I ignored it, parking it for future reference. "Well?"

"Oh, yes. Hmm. Distinguishing marks?" He thought for a moment then said, "Well, perhaps he did, there was a dark mark on his thumb. At first, I thought it was a tattoo, but now I'm not sure. Police officers aren't supposed to have tattoos showing as far as I know, so perhaps it was a birthmark, or a scar."

My heart sank. I had begun to formulate the hope that the DCI who had turned up to question me and spoke to Pascal instead, had been a fake, but the description he gave was of Garrett Blackwood and as far as I knew he was a bona fide policeman. But why would he come here and insist I was the murderer in such an unprofessional way? I couldn't figure it out and decided that as I had so little – make that none – experience of real-life policing, my naivety was causing the confusion.

Chapter Twenty-Two

The next day, with photographs returned to a tearfully grateful Marjorie, I entered the office of Babcock Publishing Limited as a temp to replace Frank Babcock's executive assistant. The story was that she had taken ill in the night and put my name forward as a substitute. I wondered how Marjorie had convinced the assistant to take the day off and then offer up a stranger in her place until I spotted a photograph on Frank's office wall. It showed his slightly plump figure in pinstripe shirt and yellow tie, belly just overhanging his belt, in the middle of a group of colleagues. To his right was a slender woman in baby pink silk shirt with flounced collar and a well-fitted below-the-knee skirt. The glossiness of her mid-length dark and curling hair reflected the light, and she looked every ounce the capable PA. Surrounded by staff in various states of joyful laughter, Frank seemed to have been caught telling a joke. The executive assistant gazed at me with laughing eyes. She was the woman from the photographs, Marjorie Babcock's lover.

As Frank introduced me to the office staff and journalists, I discovered that her name was Celia Palmer. I later discovered that she had joined the newspaper as a trainee in the typing pool and made her way up to being a secretary and then Frank's executive assistant, and had held that position for the last ten years.

Other photographs were dotted about the office, hanging on walls, and framed on desks and on top of filing cabinets. Several shelves in the office were also reserved for framed photographs, potted plants and awards, medals, and trophies. Most of the photographs on the desk were of wives, husbands, or kids whilst the ones on the walls were of Frank with various members of staff and local dignitaries, celebrities, and business leaders. It was obvious that Frank was immensely sociable at work and there were plenty of photographs of him with his staff at parties, or just chatting in the office. This surprised me. At home, Frank, though pleasant, didn't make any effort to be a friendly neighbour and sometimes seemed curmudgeonly.

After introductions to each member of the office I was shown to a desk complete with monitor and hard drive then given the passwords to access the communal digital hub and Celia's virtual workstation. The morning progressed with varying degrees of difficulty and growing anxiety. It had been twenty-six years since I last worked, and Pascal was the one with technical knowhow in our house. Content to allow him that role, I had focused on creating our home and being a dutiful, supportive wife. When the anticipated children didn't arrive, despite several attempts at IVF, Pascal had been philosophical. Turning to my garden for solace, I had been happy – most of the time – until my birthday. Now, decades later, I was digitally inept; I only had a mobile at Pascal's insistence and my activities online were pretty much restricted to purchases through Amazon and checking my bank account, which I had only just come to terms with. Working with a computer that morning was hellish, and my inability to successfully onboard with the tech seemed to be getting under Frank's skin too. After the fifth call for help, and the blunder of deleting an important file, Frank threw up his hands and left the office suite.

"Oops!" I said with a grimace as the door yawned shut on its slow-close hinge. "I think I've upset him."

My now despairing helper, Henry Vardy, a trainee journalist, and recent graduate, gave a non-committal murmur, muttered something about Frank stressing about some missing money and a meeting with the accountant, then declared the documents lost in the ether. I offered to make us both a cup of coffee and took the opportunity of escaping the hell of being shackled to the desk and checked out the multiple photographs hung around the room. A particularly large sequence showed an outing at the races, presumably Ascot, with the workers togged out in their finery; the women wore large-brimmed, flower-bedecked hats, the men wore suits and top hats. All looked supremely happy. Frank looked much younger than he had this morning, and certainly less red in the face than when he stropped out of the office, but the faces that caught my eye were of Marjorie and her lover Celia. With arms entwined around waists, each toasted the other with a bubbling flute of champagne. Frank stood at their side. The camera had caught him in a rare moment without a smile on his face, and I wondered if he knew about their affair, or was completely oblivious to the depth of the women's friendship. "Just how long have you two been together?" I whispered.

"They've been married at least thirty years." The voice startled me, and I twisted to Henry with a click of my lower vertebrae. "Kettle's boiled," he said gesturing to the kitchenette on the other side of the room.

"Sorry! Got side-tracked. Milk and sugar?" Ignoring the ache across my back, I threw him a friendly grin, and was rewarded with a grudging smile in return.

"No milk. One sugar. Thanks."

Coffee in mugs, I made my way to Henry's desk. I'd seen office-based comedies and noticed that colleagues would share gossip. some at the water fountain (there wasn't one here so that illusion was a bust), whilst others parked a thigh on the corner of the desk. Without a water fountain, I parked my thigh and a large portion of my bottom cheek on Henry's desk. The corner dug into the top of my thigh. Henry sputtered hot coffee. It dribbled down his chin and fell as a trickle onto his tie. I stood up to relieve the pain and the tension. "Sorry!"

"Did you want to talk ... or something?" He asked as he recovered, flicking at the stain on his tie.

I wanted to walk out of the office, and the building, and escape onto the street right then, but I stayed in character – it was the only way to get through the day – and asked, "So, is this the office where Selma Maybrook worked?" He threw me a suspicious glance. I was taken aback but made a quick recovery. "I'm one of her neighbours," I said, playing the sympathy card. "It was such a shock to hear about her murder! We weren't close, but still ..." I let the sentence hang in the air and made my best effort to exhibit grief, but despite trying, my eyes wouldn't tear up.

My efforts worked however, and his face softened. "Yes, she did work here. At that desk when she was in." He pointed to an empty desk with a bunch of flowers laid solemnly across the keyboard. "She's ... she was," he corrected," one of our best writers." He motioned to a framed award. "That's for Newspaper of the Year, an Industry Gold Award, but it was Selma's work that really got it for us."

"She must have been popular then?"

"Hah! No." he said this without thought and instantly looked regretful. "I mean ... I didn't mean to speak ill of her, not now she's dead, but ... well, she was ambitious, and ambitious people sometimes tread on others to get up that greasy ladder." He took a sip of coffee. "There are at least three people I know of who won't be crying any tears at her funeral."

"Oh?"

"Well," he said with a quick glance around the room, "there's Mandy Sanderson." He gave a subtle nod towards a woman just leaving the office. "She joined the paper when Selma did, apparently, and they even worked together on a couple of articles, but they fell out big time when Selma accused Mandy of stealing her research for an article about a corrupt local bank manager. Mandy denied it, but the mud stuck, and Frank never trusted her again. Then there's Alistair Collings. They say she got him sacked. Whatever the truth is, he left and now works at a rival paper, but he had to take a massive salary cut to get the job."

"Who's the third then?"

"That would be Carl Jacques. They were friends with benefits if you know what I mean." Henry offered me a wink. "But get this, he was married!"

"That's awful!" I said as though surprised. "I never would have imagined she'd do that!"

"Hah! That's the half of it. Anyway, this Carl Jacques was earmarked for promotion, and then Selma made a play for the job too. Guess what? Selma got the job, and the hefty pay rise. Carl left the next day, and he's not even a journo anymore. Works in car sales or something."

"That's terrible!"

He nodded. "The word on the grapevine is that she blackmailed him—said she'd tell his wife if he took the job."

"It makes you wonder then, who killed her."

"It does. My money is on someone she'd piss- ... ticked off."

"You don't think that it was a robbery gone wrong, then? It's what we're all worried about down the street."

"I doubt it. Her latest story was going to be her most explosive yet. I think she actually liked winding people up."

I recalled the abusive emails. "Hmm. Must have been a corker of a story. Any idea what it was about?"

"I don't know, all I know is that she was working with Simon on it until a few weeks ago and then they fell out."

"Simon?"

"Yeah, poor sod died last week. They only buried him the day before Selma died."

Simon! The man whose funeral she had been so cut up about, the man whose wife accused Selma of being responsible for his death. "Do you think their deaths are related?"

"No! Why would they be? Simon died in a car crash on his way back from meeting a contact, and Selma died of poisoning—that's the word anyway."

It was the first time I'd heard of what had actually killed Selma, or Simon. In my mind's eye, the attacker had suffocated her with a pillow, or strangled her with a dressing gown cord.

That she had been poisoned put a whole new spin on it. The poison could have been working its way through her body when I helped her to bed! "Poisoned?"

"Yeah, and you know what they say about poisoning ..."

"No!"

"Women! Loads of cases of wives poisoning men, particularly their husbands."

"But Selma was a woman."

He threw me a confused frown. "She was ... Not a bad way to go, though. Some poisons take you quick."

"So, you know what kind of poison killed Selma?"

"... No, actually I don't. It was just something I heard one of the office girls say."

So only gossip, and possibly not true! "Hmm. So, who do you think poisoned Selma? I'm worried now that we've got a killer in the Close! What if they come back?" I attempted to channel fear. "I only live up the road, perhaps ... I could be next!" He offered me a concerned glance with a sprinkling of pity, and I congratulated myself on my performance; my acting skills really weren't too bad.

He paused, then said, "I have no idea, and I doubt there's a serial-killing poisoner on the loose. If I was doing the job of finding out who killed her, I'd be checking out her latest investigation and having a chat with her informant."

I had nothing to lose, and unashamedly asked, "And who would that be?"

Henry's brows creased, and then his lips thinned. "I have no idea." It was obvious I'd overstepped the mark, perhaps even sparked suspicion, and with the conversation at an end, he gestured to my desk and added, "Don't you have work to do?"

Inwardly I groaned at the thought of attempting to work with more digital files. Outwardly I offered him a broad smile, making no sign of being offended by his brusqueness and, for the remainder of the day, continued to grapple with the computer and the paperwork handed to me. I limped on and sighed with relief when my hours at the office came to an end.

As everyone left, I busied myself with imaginary paperwork, and then made my way to the ladies. When a cleaner came in, I found a walk-in cupboard and hid there until I was sure no one was left on our floor of the building. Certain that everyone had gone home for the day, and that I wouldn't be detected, I returned to the office and Selma's desk.

Chapter Twenty-Three

Early evening sun filtered through the window as I entered the open plan office but, with the air conditioning set to an uncomfortably low level, the room was chilly. Despite the potted plants and framed photographs dotted about, the room seemed sterile. Beige walls dominated and weren't complimented by the blocky veneered MDF desks and heavy-duty, dirt-resistant royal blue carpet. Feeling thankful not to have to spend my days locked in the soulless box, I made a beeline for Selma's desk.

The flowers placed across her keyboard had been abandoned in the kitchenette's sink. Her personal effects, two framed photographs of herself with celebrity writers, and a withered supermarket aloe vera plant, were stacked on the counter. Sitting in her chair, I stared at the blank monitor, unsure of quite what to do. Exploring Selma's files had seemed like a great idea in theory, but in practice I wasn't sure quite how to go about it. Remembering the induction from the morning, I switched the hard drive on. The monitor blinked and the screen became bright blue. Tapping in the communal access code got me through to another screen demanding Selma's password. I had no idea what that was. I tried a few variations of her name along the lines of Celia's password, but all to no effect. The screen flashed a warning that I had one more attempt remaining before being blocked for several hours.

Sitting back in the chair, tension rising along with the clatter of equipment and doors as the cleaning crew I thought had left, worked through the building, I stared at the screen and decided to use magic. I had no idea what to do. The charm my aunts had told me to recite to help vanquish an enemy was useless in this instance. However, alone in the office, my curiosity piqued, I decided to try it.

Searching for something suitable to work the magic on, the flowers protruding from the sink caught my eye. The thought of making those beautiful blooms 'shrink like dung' didn't sit well with me, so I looked for another object. A folder on a nearby desk was the only thing I could find. I focused my attention on it and repeated the spell. First, I tried it in modern English, "... May you shrink away like dung." Nothing happened. Next, I spoke it in an older form, the language of our ancestors, "... Scring þu alswa scerne awage". The words were awkward, my tongue unused to speaking them. I watched the folder intently, but there was no change in its size. Disappointed and feeling a little foolish, I turned back to the screen. I wasn't ready to give up. If magic wouldn't work on the book, it may work on something a little more 'alive'.

Focusing on creating a spell that would magically unlock the password protected file, I thought hard for a moment then muttered a rhyme. Like my other efforts at rhyming, it was diabolical, but they had worked and this one might just do the trick. I recited the charm, this time with a little more confidence. The monitor blinked dumbly back, goading me with the threat of being locked out after one more failed attempt. On another floor I heard a man laugh and a door close. The voice sounded closer than before and panic set in. Fingers hovering over the keyboard, I muttered with frustration. "Open up, damned folder, before I get a second older! Show me the key, so that I may see!"

The screen flickered and the threatening message disappeared and, for one joyous second, I believed that this new and demanding rhyme had worked. But, with malice, the device switched to sleep mode.

Frustrated, but still determined to find some clue that would help me get a step closer to solving the murder, I decided to leave the computer files for a few minutes before a final attempt, and turned my attention to Selma's desk. There were three drawers. I pulled at the first only to discover it was locked. "Damn!" I whispered. My sleuthing was getting me nowhere fast! Between the top drawer and the desk there was a gap just big enough to hide a few folders, a book, or a set of keys. I slid my hand into the gap to check if a key had been hidden. The space was empty. I had one more avenue to try. I knew that Pascal kept a spare key for his office desk taped beneath the bottom drawer. Crouching, then lowering to my knees, and then on all fours, I swept my hand beneath the bottom drawer, puffing with the effort and regretting the extra pounds I needed to lose. The tip of my finger touched something metallic "Gotcha!" I slid my arm as far as possible beneath the desk, bottom to the heavens, and pickled at the tape-held key.

Behind me footsteps padded.

"Well, that is a sight I'd rather not see!"

Startled by the voice, and intensely aware of my generous bottom pointing skyward, I jerked, trapped my arm against the drawer and caught my head on the edge of the desk. Pain shot through the top of my skull as the desk's metal frame hit my head and dug into the soft flesh of my inner elbow.

"Lucifer!" I scolded through my pain. "You startled me!" I swear the feline chuckled as he sidled from behind then sat inches from my face; the cat had no respect for personal space unless it was his own! "Don't you know that it's customary to announce your arrival? Perhaps a knock, or even a cough from the doorway would help? Maybe a call of 'hello!'" Annoyed at being startled, and in pain, I was less than friendly.

Lucifer simply stared back with those huge, and deeply knowing, eyes. "And where would be the fun in that, pray tell? By the way, you might like to lower your rear end!"

A tinge of embarrassment added to the flush on my already reddened cheeks. The tape holding the key released and I pulled myself out from under the desk and held it up in triumph then turned my attention to Lucifer. "What are you doing here?"

"I've come to help, Liv, but now I'm wishing I hadn't bothered." He tipped his nose upwards and averted his eyes. "I'm beginning to feel ... unwanted, to tell you the truth. You're never there for me; not since your birthday. And you're always leaving me behind. It's as if ... It's as if you don't want me around ... now you've met the *real* me!"

It was true. I found the new Lucifer 'unimproved' and was fed up with his disparaging comments. In truth, he made me feel uneasy, and a little inadequate. "Don't be silly!" I was thrown by how close to the truth he was. "Of course I'm always here for you." He continued to ignore me. "It's just taking some getting used to – having a talking cat – but I still ... love you."

That was also true. He continued to hold himself aloof but cast a disdainful glance at the key in my hand.

"What's that for?" He asked as I pulled off the remaining tape.

"It's a key to Selma's desk."

"She kept it in the same place that Pascal keeps his?"

"That's right."

"So, you deduced that the key might be there too."

"I did."

"Good."

Was that a compliment? With a smile, I turned to the desk and unlocked the drawer. It was arranged in similar fashion to the one at Selma's home – stationery in the top, notebooks in the second drawer, and an identical hardback book hidden beneath larger folders in the bottom. Removing it proved that Selma had been methodical, if not predictable. An identical manilla folder was taped to the back. One side, however, was unsealed. Lucifer jumped up onto the desk as I shook out the contents. Several photographs, a memory stick, and some papers slipped onto the surface.

The photographs showed a group of people in front of a gate against a backdrop of rolling green hills spotted with sheep. Most looked equipped for a trek in thick fleeces, rucksacks, and walking poles, whilst others wore wellingtons, and some were in flat caps. To one side was a large sign with 'Property of Gazcon Oil & Gas Corp. Trespassers will be prosecuted. No liability accepted for injury or death.' Below this was an image of an armed security officer with a large Alsatian. Many in the group were holding placards daubed with 'Frack-Off Gazcon!' and 'Save Our Heritage'.

I examined their faces. There were several women in the group, and I recognised one despite the woollen beanie pulled down to her eyebrows. It was Selma Maybrook. In another photograph taken at the same site, but without protesters, Selma appeared again. This was a more formal photograph and she was pictured shaking a Gazcon executive's hand. A folded newspaper was held for the camera to record the headline, 'Gazcon Investment Lands 200 Local Jobs'.

"Up to no good as usual, Selma!" I said. It was obvious to me what she was doing. Infiltrating the protestors then brown-nosing with the men with the money. "No change there then!"

The pictured article was also saved in the stash. It was dry and lacked the usual enthusiasm of Selma's work. Along with the photos were several clippings from what looked like broadsheet newspapers, and one had the distinctive pink of the Financial Times. All the articles related to Gazcon Oil & Gas Corp and its heavy investment in fracking. Another mentioned the government's turnaround on fracking after a series of earthquakes. I sighed. It was a dead-end. If fracking had been stopped, then there was no need for protest, or disrupting it. However, I continued to glance through the material. Several anti-fracking articles by a May Brook were clipped out too. The articles were old, and it seemed that the fracking company had halted operations at the heritage site.

As I sifted through the remaining pieces, a slim sheaf of stapled paper made me sit up. It was an unpublished piece, an article claiming that fracking had been given the go ahead by ministers behind closed doors. Corruption at the highest levels was suggested along with aggressive foreign influence. The article was co-authored by Simon Brentwood and May Brook and was dated to a week before Simon was killed. Various notes were written in the margins, some with commentary by another hand. On the last page was a handwritten note signed by Simon agreeing to several points in the article. Attached to the back was a post-it-note in Simon's hand. 'Going to meet Svetlana Gurchenko at Heargholtsby Hill. She has details about the application.' The note was dated the day of his death. One other article was included, this one printed from a website, with the title, 'New Gold – Fracking Companies on the Verge of Prosperity'. It was dated a month before my birthday and listed Gazcon Oil & Gas Corp as among the companies reaping the enormous rewards of fracking.

For a moment I couldn't understand why Selma had an unpublished copy of May Brook's damning article. It took a few moments before I realised why the name seemed familiar. May Brook *was* Selma Maybrook!

Selma Maybrook, the pro-fracking journalist who had written a dry piece trumpeting Gazcon's investment into the local economy was also May Brook, the anti-fracking journalist who had written a vivid and passionate article with supporting, possibly career destroying, evidence of widespread corruption within the industry and in local and national government.

I realised then that the reason she was in the anti-fracking photograph wasn't because she was attempting to sabotage the protesters, but because she *was* a protester! "Well, Selma!" I said with growing admiration for the despised woman. "I never took you for an eco-warrior!" I stopped for a moment, staring down at the photograph of Selma the protester, and felt a surge of pity. "Is that why you and Simon are dead?" Two minutes of researching on my mobile produced the information I needed.

Simon had died only twenty miles from the protested fracking site. "Someone murdered Simon too, Lucifer. I'm sure of it, and I bet it was the same person who killed Selma."

With a curl of his tail, Lucifer sauntered to the door. "It's time we were going."

The voices heard earlier were close and, not wanting to be discovered, I collected the evidence, popped it into my bag, and slipped out of the building. Tomorrow I would make my way to the fracking site and see for myself if it were secretly operational.

Chapter Twenty-Four

Worn out by the stress of the day – dealing with technology had taken all my energy – I fell asleep on my hotel bed with the evidence (clippings, print outs, photographs, and post-it note) spread out on the cover. I woke twice in the night. First as papers fell to the floor with a thud, and the second drenched in sweat with a sense of foreboding that the room was closing in on me. I don't recall a nightmare, but, like my own house, the energy in the room seemed dark and oppressive. Heart palpitating and drenched in sweat, I searched the room's shadows. Grey light filtered through the curtains making the room dingey rather than dark. There was no one in the room with me, but I couldn't shake the feeling of being watched. I checked the time on my mobile; the screen showed 03:55. It was already growing light and although still groggy I knew I wouldn't be able to sleep. Falling asleep didn't seem to be too much of a problem these days but staying asleep was something else! On the plus side, I was growing used to the earlier mornings, and enjoying them.

I showered, dressed, made myself a coffee, restacked the evidence then sifted through it again as my hair dried and the sun rose.

An hour later, I was much better informed. Gazcon Oil and Gas Corp had bought the rights to drill at Heargholtsby

Hill, a place of outstanding natural beauty beside an isolated village deep in the English countryside. An ancient woodland, a place that protesters claimed was also a place of pagan worship and sacred, was at the very edge of where the company wanted to drill and was marked for clearing. Despite protests and pleas from anti-frackers and the pagan community, the government had granted the drilling licence. The earthmovers had arrived, a huge fence erected, and destruction of the area had begun almost immediately. The woodlands and pagan shrine site had only been saved by the government's U-turn on fracking. I could find nothing on the recommencement of fracking at the site anywhere on the web. Gazcon's website made no mention of fracking operations. What I did find on the website were several photographs of Ivan Schofield, Gazcon's CEO shaking hands with Turkey's Minister for the Environment and another with him at a charity ball.

I typed in 'Ivan Schofield CEO Gazcon' chose the 'image' option, and scrolled through more than fifty photographs where he featured. Many of them showed him shaking hands with dignitaries at various Ministries across the globe and various charity events and green energy conferences. In one he was seen at an anti-carbon rally and appeared to be among the crowd of protesters. This image intrigued me. He certainly looked younger in the photo, not quite a student, but at least a decade younger than his current photographs. Clicking the link sent me to a page that wouldn't load. After several attempts to follow this lead, I gave up, assuming some issue with my mobile's connection. I refreshed my browser and continued to scroll through the photographs.

With only a few remaining, a figure at the edge of one caught my eye. Frank Babcock! I zoomed in. Yes! It was him. The image was of another charity ball, this time one I was aware of. The charity was Marjorie Babcock's pet project, and each year she would throw a ball to help raise funds. Only the wealthy and powerful were invited and photographs from the evening, of men in black tie, and women in ball gowns, would invariably appear in the local paper and the glossy 'high-society' magazines the company also published.

"That's why you wrote the article as May Brook" I said aloud. "Frank Babcock was one of Gazcon's cronies!"

I followed the link from the photograph to the newspaper article it accompanied. It linked to the online version of the paper under their 'Society' section. It was a dead end, so I scrolled through their 'Environment' section. There were no articles relating to Gazcon, or the fracking site. Turning to the 'Business & Finance' section, the only article was the online version where Selma was shown shaking hands with the CEO. It was identical to the clipping in the folder lauding the investment and jobs brought to the region by Gazcon, detailing the job creation scheme, the input of potential investment in local infrastructure: new roads, a school annexe, and a list of local businesses that would be receiving grants from their 'community pot'. "Hush money!" I whispered. It was obvious to me now that the company had bribed the local community, council, and the media, to damp down the opposition to the fracking before the government U-turn.

It had also become obvious that Simon and Selma had been killed to shut them up about the company's new activities.

I tried once more to follow the link from the photograph of the CEO as protestor. The link only buffered. All other links had connected to their source. Despite my lack of internet savvy, I became suspicious and there was only one person I knew who could help me. Pascal. I called him, explained the situation and what I had found, and ended our conversation with a sense of dark foreboding. It took someone with deep pockets and serious connections to influence internet search engines, he had said. His last words to me had been to forget trying to be a detective and get myself home. I ignored him, packed my bag, checked out of the hotel, punched the fracking site's directions into the Satnav, and left town. I had to talk to Svetlana Gurchenko. If she was still alive.

I had no idea of the danger I was walking into, but I was about to find out.

Chapter Twenty-Five

Heargholtsby lay in the opposite direction of Heligern Cottage where my aunts were awaiting my return for the Solstice. As I travelled along, I wondered how they would manage in the shop. As far as I knew, they only sold their products in the village, but taking premises would require business rates to be paid along with utilities, and the footfall the village offered would not cover those bills. As I continued my journey, my thoughts full of Heligern, the forthcoming initiation, and my aunts, I realised that I would have to help them with this new project—once I'd been cleared of murder of course!

An hour later, having left the major roads behind and travelling down a road so narrow that only one car, or tractor, would fit, I arrived at Heargholtsby. Nestled within a valley, the village spread along the base of undulating hills. On a steeper slope, a single farmhouse sat in isolation. A river crossed by a stone bridge, ran alongside the main street.

I drove through the village, noting the chapel, two shops, and an alehouse. The houses were a mixture of vintage, old, and ancient, and, at least along the main street, nothing appeared to have been built since 1930. Both shops, one a butcher-cum-baker, the other a post-office-cum-general supplies store, were open. Their striped awnings, pulled down to shield the windows from an already hot sun, were unfaded and obviously new. The shops, I decided, would be my first stop, followed by the alehouse, but before I spoke to the villagers, I wanted to drive through the village to get a feel for the place.

As I passed a short row of stone-built terraced cottages, I noticed a small hand-made poster. It was printed with 'Stop the Fracking' in sun-faded ink. In another garden a weathered placard similar in size to a 'for sale' sign, lay uprooted and propped against a hedge. It too had a faded anti-fracking message.

I travelled to the outskirts of the village, passing a playground and then the village school. The playground was well-equipped, the climbing frame, swings, and roundabout painted in bright primary colours. The rubber matting beneath was black, unfaded by the sun, not greened by lichen nor sprinkled with clumps of moss like the ones in my local playground. As with the shops' awnings, the playground equipment was new. Beside the play area construction workers were busy at the school, replacing windows and building a small annexe. Closer to the centre of the village, the chapel was being given a new slate roof, and I counted at least three houses where extensions were under construction.

At the alehouse there was no sign of building work, but a gleaming Rolls Royce and a vintage Aston Martin were parked in the car park. As I motored down another picturesque lane, I found my way blocked by yet another builder's truck, this one laden with oak beams. The view to the back garden of the house at which they were working, showed a large structure being erected. In the front drive of the house, which looked in need of renovation, an old car, its red paintwork sun worn, sat beside a gleaming Audi TT Roadster, the exact car Pascal had been mooning over last month. I knew then that whoever lived in the shabby house had been paid off. The car was the latest model and cost upwards of £35,000. As I motored through the picturesque lanes, all the evidence pointed to a sudden injection of cash. My heart sank a little; if the villagers had been paid off, and were now colluding with the oil and gas company, anyone who had evidence of corruption, like Simon, Selma, and possibly Svetlana, could be a target. It also meant that any one of the villagers may have been tempted to murder.

Reaching the end of the lane, I did a three-point turn and returned to the main street, determined to talk to the villagers; I had to find Svetlana—hopefully alive!

My first port of call was the General Store. Inside, it was obvious that the shop had undergone a recent refurbishment. Chrome fittings gleamed against the cream backboards of floor to ceiling shelving. A young girl appeared from the side of an overlarge central aisle that dominated the space. Can of beans in hand she called, "Shop!" through an open doorway then offered me a friendly smile.

"Just coming!" a man's voice returned.

I busied myself looking at a rack of magazines whilst I waited for the 'shop' to arrive, presuming it would be the owner, or manager. Seconds later, brushing crumbs from his shirt, he sidled to the counter, squeezing himself behind the cash register. A large man, he stood at least six-foot tall with broad shoulders. Filled out to paunch, his grizzled beard was peppered with the first signs of grey. I estimated him to be around forty years old. Deciding against any of the magazines on offer, I picked a chocolate bar from the counter. Then replaced it. This seemed to irk the man and his flicker of annoyance put me on edge. I scanned the shop for something to buy that wouldn't add to my waistline and grabbed a bottle of water from the front of the counter. The air in the small shop was already heating up and the plastic bottle felt warm to the touch.

"Is that everything, love?"

"Yes, thanks!" I hoped my smile would earn me at least one brownie point and offered him a five-pound note. As he opened the till for change, I took a breath. "So," I said in my best I'm-not-really-interested voice. "Looks like there's a lot of work going on in the village."

He ignored me as he counted the change.

I tried again. "I noticed they've put a new playground in, and the school's getting an extra classroom."

"It's not a new classroom," the young girl explained. "It's a dinner hall. We didn't have one before. When I was at school, we had to eat our pack-up in the classroom."

"Oh, well that's a nice improvement," I offered. The girl at least, was warming to me. "And there's lots of other work too—around the village. Quite a few houses are having work done. And your shop," I gestured to the new fittings. "Looks lovely. Is it all new?"

By now I had the man's full attention, and it wasn't particularly friendly. "Fairly new," he admitted.

"We had it all put in last month. You should have seen the mess they made! There was dust everywhere. I had to clean everything!"

"You were paid!" the man snipped.

The girl's mouth pursed shut and she returned to stacking he shelves. Ignoring the man's gruff response, I asked the question I really wanted an answer to. "So, I'm looking for an old friend." I took a swig of the tepid water in an effort to appear nonchalant. "Her name's Svetlana Gurchenko. Do you know her? I can't seem to locate her house."

Silence filled the shop. The girl flinched, met my eyes, and was about to speak when the man said. "Nope. Can't help you. We don't know anyone called Svetlana."

The girl flushed and disappeared behind the central aisle.

My instincts told me the shopkeeper was lying, but I went along with the charade. "Oh, well, that's a shame. She's an old friend, and I thought I'd look her up, but I must have mis-remembered her address."

"Yeah, I think you must. Maybe the next village on? It's got a similar name."

"That must be it!" I thanked him again for the water and left the shop, certain he knew Svetlana, or at least knew of her.

My next stop was the butcher-cum-baker three doors down. Like the general store, the shop had undergone a recent refit. The cool air within was a welcome relief from the increasing heat outside. Anxiety swirled within me, and that familiar heat was rising from my belly, sweat began to trickle down my spine. *Not now, Liv! Keep it under control.* With a calming breath I smiled at the butcher and purchased a link of sausages, a large pork pie, and two Cornish pasties. I knew the aunts loved pork pies, and I could eat one of the pasties for lunch, at least it would have some vegetables in it. The sausages were a mistake in the heat, they'd be high before I got them home.

With the fizzing sensation in my fingers ebbing, but with sweat beginning to bead at my hairline, I complimented the butcher on the shop's new interior. He responded with professional courtesy. After the conversation with the shopkeeper, I watched the butcher's face carefully as he answered my questions. A flicker in his eye was quickly hidden when I mentioned Svetlana's name.

"No, sorry Miss, I can't help you."

Can't or won't? I decided to push a little. "So, you don't know her?"

He faltered, caught my gaze, then turned his attention to butchering a rack of lamb. His meat cleaver chopped down, and a lamb chop cleaved neatly from the rack and toppled onto the wooden board. A blush had risen to his cheeks. "I told you, I can't help you, Miss." His hand trembled.

Convinced that the butcher and the shopkeeper were both lying, I left the shop more convinced that Svetlana had met the same fate as Simon and Selma.

I had one more place to try—the alehouse.

The Aston Martin's metallic baby blue paintwork glittered in the sun as I stepped through the doors of the ancient tavern. Inside was like stepping back in time. Dark wooden panels carved with flowers and roundels lined the walls. A huge fireplace dominated one end of the room; its brickwork blackened. The fire itself was held by an iron grate in the hearth, the ashes spilling through to the large flagstones beneath. At the back a massive fire plate was moulded with a scene of dragons. The seating was a mixture of worn pine benches, high-backed grandfather chairs, and shorter captain's chairs. The tables were small and round, or rectangular, and the air was pungent with the odour of stale beer and pipe tobacco. There were no customers, but one table had been laid out with cutlery and serviettes and a small placeholder printed with 'Reserved' sat beside a vase of lavender and roses at the centre.

Behind the bar, a woman dried a glass and placed it beneath the counter. As I approached her the door opened and an old man shuffled in.

"Morning, Alf!" she called then turned her attention to me. "What can I get you, love?"

With the morning coming to a close, and still no closer to finding Svetlana, I dispensed with efforts to curry favour and said, "I'm looking for Svetlana Gurchenko."

The old man shuffled to a stop. "The Russian lass that took Gantry's cottage?"

This was it!

"Sorry, love." The woman's voice boomed across the pub, obviously for Alf's benefit. "We don't know anyone of that name here."

"Rose Cottage," Alf supplied. "I thought it were a Russian lass that lived there."

"No, Alf, love! It were a Polish couple ... Remember? Irena and Lukas Romanov ... Polanski."

Romanov Polanski? For a moment I believed her, but quickly realised she was lying too. Romanov was the family name of the Russian royal family deposed, and disposed of, during the revolution in 1917.

"No, Lizzie. She *were* a Russian. I distinctly remember she said she fought at Stalingrad. Forty kills she had, that's what she told me. She was a sniper during the war."

My hope faded.

"Fought at Stalingrad?" Lizzie asked with genuine bemusement, then laughed. "A woman sniper? Oh, Alf! You are confused! That was a long, long time ago." She shook her head then lowered her voice. "Poor old Alf's going a bit senile. He thinks the war's still on!" She tutted. "Poor bugger. We all keep an eye on him though. It's a tightknit village; we look after each other."

With that line of enquiry at a dead end, I left and walked a little further through the village, then considered returning to the pub for a cold drink in the beer garden and a bite of my Cornish pasty. Checking my watch showed it to be nearly one o'clock, and I shelved that idea. The day was already half over, the Solstice was tomorrow, and I still hadn't cleared my name!

Now certain that Svetlana, my only lead, had come to a sticky end, I set out to find 'Rose Cottage'.

Chapter Twenty-Six

As I walked towards the outskirts of the village, hoping to find Rose Cottage, the shopkeeper strode past me. He was in a hurry and already out of breath. Ignoring me as he brushed past, he made his way to the old chapel ahead. He stopped in front of the large noticeboard erected on wooden posts behind the chapel's low stone wall and held a key at the glass doors. Clumsy fingers slowed him down and he dropped the keys in his haste.

Interest piqued, I increased my pace, pulling myself back from a run, and caught up with him just as he unlocked the glass panels. He manoeuvred himself to block my view of the noticeboard and as a glass door swung open, he grasped at a pinned leaflet. All consideration of personal space gone, I pushed up beside him to peer over his arm at the paper. His hand crumpled round it before I had a chance to read the printed text, but I managed a glance. It appeared to be hand-written. I noticed the word 'fracking' and '7pm'. There was also what could be a telephone number and the letters 'SVE'. With a grunt he stepped back and relocked the door.

Emboldened by the knowledge that he was deliberately hiding the leaflet from me, and determined to see it in full, I asked, "Can I see it?" and held out my hand.

Without meeting my gaze, he sidestepped me, his fist clenched around the paper. "No!"

The end of the leaflet poked out from his closed fist. I tried to grab it, but he pulled his hand from my reach with a jerk and took a massive stride back towards the shop. Certain that the flyer was another clue, I had to see what was written there. With massive effort I focused. Heat swirled at my core as I concentrated on his clenched fist. *Open your hand. Drop the paper!* He strode away, oblivious to my efforts. My fingers fizzed. The air around my hands crackled. *Drop the paper!* His figure diminished as the distance between us grew. Sparks flew from my hands, crackling and fizzing as they struck the ground. I sensed the energy building and just as I reached a point so hot that I thought I might explode, I silently shouted 'Stop!'. The man continued to walk, but from somewhere within, an unfamiliar voice rose. "Take heed false toad else I will throw thee into the road," I called. "Open thy fist, unfurl thy hand. Give me the paper or live breathless beneath the land!" I muttered this in a growling and threatening voice. Simultaneously shocked that I had threatened the man's life and confused as to where the words had come from, I stood mesmerised as he began to react to the command. As the words 'breathless beneath the land' left my mouth, sparks had shot from my fingers and were now dancing on the man's back. Purple, pink, silver, and shining black particles crackled and fizzed in a haze of brilliance that hovered around his body. He staggered to a stop, unfurled his hand, and dropped the paper on the path.

Make haste, Livitha! Takest thy reward. The unfamiliar voice whispered in my ear and I took a quick glance round to locate it. Realising I was alone on the path, disturbed by the voice and amazed at the control my chaotic energy had over the man, I ran for the paper, catching it just as a gust of wind lifted it from the ground. The man shivered, shook his head, then walked back to his shop without a backwards glance.

The paper was a notice about a meeting. The address was for Rose Cottage, Piggery Hill, Heargholtsby. All were welcome. It was complete with a mobile number and a name, Svetlana Gurchenko.

From this I deduced that Rose Cottage was sited on one of the steep and winding roads that led out of the village. I returned to my car and began the search for Svetlana's house.

Ten minutes later, midway up Piggery Hill, Svetlana's isolated cottage sat before me. Roses grew in abundance over trellis either side of a quaint porch of lichen-covered tiles and oak posts. A worn brick path edged by bright lavender led to the front door. The cottage itself was squat and painted white over lime render. Around the edges of twin lawns, snap dragons swayed with foxgloves in the generous borders, and the serrated petals of vibrant pinks sat beside creamy white geraniums. The garden was alive with movement as bees buzzed from flower to flower. But the curtains were drawn shut, and the windows stared dumbly at me as I took the path to the door.

No one answered my knock.

Going round to the back of the house revealed a patio area with a table and chairs. Beyond that was a large lawned area, again edged by deep borders filled with foxgloves, snapdragons, hollyhocks, lavender, geraniums, and roses. At its bottom, the garden opened out to a small orchard. The space was beautiful, just the kind of garden I could spend my entire year working in.

After a moment of intense desire, I turned my attention back to finding Svetlana.

It was immediately obvious that something was wrong.

A cardigan was draped over the back of a chair. A book lay beneath the wrought iron table, its pages ruckled and swollen with rain from last night's downpour. A large and well-made parasol was slotted through the middle of the patio table. Fully open, it was skewed at an angle, its fabric damaged. The garden was obviously loved, the items well cared for, and I doubted that Svetlana would leave the obviously expensive parasol outside. Open, and at the mercy of last night's summer storm, it would inevitably become damaged—as it had.

Out of sight of the road, and without neighbours to overlook the back garden, I knocked on the back door. When the knock remained unanswered, I tried the handle and was surprised when it lowered with ease and the latch clicked. I opened the door a fraction and called a tentative, 'Hello!' My call also went unanswered and from the energy within the house I sensed it was unoccupied. The back door led immediately into the kitchen. The ripe smell and buzz of flies hit me first. Scanning the kitchen, evidence remained of food preparation on the counter. A loaf of bread sat on a wooden board. Two slices had been cut and laid beside the loaf. There was no sign of the breadknife. Flies buzzed around a bowl and the pungent odour of tinned tuna wafted to me. Tomatoes, peppers, and a handful of wilted spinach sat prepared on another chopping board. It seemed to me that Svetlana had been in the middle of making a tuna sandwich, probably her lunch, when she had been interrupted. I took another step into the room and my foot kicked against an object that skittled across the floor. The breadknife hit the kickboard then rebounded. The blade was dulled, and closer inspection revealed dried smears of blood. Thicker globules had coagulated along its edge.

Noise from outside caught my attention as I crouched to the knife. I didn't try to pick it up, touching it would leave fingerprints that could be used as damning evidence if an investigation took a wrong turn—as Selma's had.

Several seconds passed as I listened for the noise. It didn't repeat, and the only sounds were the thrum of a distant engine and the chitter of birds in the garden. A skewed kitchen table and an upturned chair were other signs of a struggle in the kitchen. There were also several spots of blood that trailed to the back door. I imagined the scenario; Svetlana had taken a break from reading and was happily making her lunch, no doubt listening to the birds with the back door open to allow fresh air to cool the house, when masked attackers charged through the door. They grabbed her from behind, taking her by surprise, but she just had time to grab the breadknife. A struggle followed and one of the attackers, or Svetlana herself, had been injured. Her efforts had been in vain and she had been taken, abducted to meet a foul and murderous end! With my inner voice once again narrating events in a deep and hyperbolic voice, I turned from the upturned chair and skewed table just in time to see a dark figure pass the window.

Within the next second the dark figure stood in the doorway, the bright sun casting the man in silhouette.

I screamed.

The figure lurched over the threshold.

I took a step back knocking into the sink.

"Now, now lass! Steady on."

The relief was immense. I recognised the voice. It was Alf, the senile old man from the ale house.

"I din't mean to scare thee."

"You didn't! ... well, you did, but it's alright." Suddenly aware that I was trespassing in a stranger's home I scrabbled for an excuse. "My friend ... she lives here. I just popped by to say hello."

"Weel, tha's wull not find her heer."

"No, I mean, yes. I can see that she's not here." He caught my gaze with rheumy, questioning eyes. "I should go. I'll call her later. Maybe leave a note."

"She's bin taken."

This admission stopped me in my tracks. "Taken? Svetlana?"

"Aye. The Russian lass. They took her."

"I knew it! No one leaves tuna out to stink up a house."

"Aye. And there's a bloodied knife on the floor too."

"Aye ... I mean, there is. I kicked it, but I haven't touched it."

"Good lass. Thas dirrin't want them poleece getting to wrong thinking now. Dos't tha."

"No!" I certainly did not; being the prime suspect in one murder was quite enough!

"Them in the village think I'm too old to notice, but I see!" He tapped at his temple. "I see everything."

I gave an encouraging nod.

"The lass wouldn't be quiet, so they shut her up."

"They bribed her?"

"Nay lass. The shut her up, they did. In a box."

A cold shiver ran down my spine. "A box?"

"Aye. On the back of a truck it were. Like a big fridge it was, but I saw them bundle her in there." He tapped the side of his temple again. "They think I'm too old to notice, but I see. She were staggering, with tape across her mouth."

The man seemed lucid enough, the 'senility' seen at the alehouse possibly a front.

"Do you think it's the Russians come to get her?" My belief in him began to waver. "She said they would. Maybe she's a soviet spy and the Brits knobbled her?" He said this with a glint in his eye, and I could tell he was enjoying the excitement.

My hope sank a little. Unsure whether he was senile and living in a fantasy, or was perfectly sane and recounting events, I asked. "Where's the box?"

He shrugged. "I dunno. They drove her away on the back of the truck, but I've see'd that truck afore. It goes up that hill." He gestured to the lane that led out of the village.

"Piggery Hill?" I clarified.

"Aye. But tha dostn't want to go up that hill lass, tha might not come back down."

"What's up the hill, Alf?"

Chapter Twenty-Seven

Walking back to the car left me breathless, but twenty minutes after entering her home I motored past Selma's cottage on my way to the top of Piggery Hill with Alf's directions to the fracking site scrawled in his unsteady hand. Watching him draw the map and label the lanes and turnoffs had stabbed at my heart. His hand shook, but it was obvious that he had once been a strong man, and his writing, learnt as a boy, a curling copperplate. I thought then of Aunt Loveday and her efforts to keep her soulmate alive. Uncle Raif, still generally sprightly, was showing signs of advanced age. Worryingly, he had been uncharacteristically unwell and a little frail of late. One day, he too would be like Alf, fragile with the countdown towards the grave measured in years and months rather than centuries and decades.

The fracking site was a surprise. I had expected it to be an area of scraped earth and rolling earth movers, men with hard hats and stacked portacabins like the images I had seen of other sites. Here there was no sign of activity. The earth showed signs of being ravaged, and across an open space great grooves had been gouged into the soil, but these were already overgrown with grass. Beyond the cleared area was a bank of forest that spread out across the hillside and down into the valley beyond.

Grass nodded on long stems in the warm afternoon sun as I clicked my car to locked. The terrain in the clearing was uneven and I regretted not wearing my walking boots. However, there was fresh sign of activity where newly grown grass had been churned by thick tyres, too wide and heavy to be made by a car. Someone had been here in the last day or so. The grass, though flattened, wasn't browning or wilted, and the churned mud, despite the heat, still appeared wet. Someone could have passed through the gate this morning. Determined to investigate further, and with the only access to the site over a high metal gate, I climbed the bars, puffing as I swung my leg over the top. The gate wobbled as I straddled it and I couldn't help a small squeak of fear as I wavered. With my grip tight, I eased myself slowly over the top, jumping down the last foot to the ground. It was then that I saw the paper pinned to a tree—on the other side of the gate!

It had to be important. I climbed back over the gate.

The paper was a single piece of laminated A4 and was an announcement for the application of planning permission to build seventy executive five-bedroom dwellings on the land. Dated two months ago, any objections had to be submitted by next week. My heart sank. It was obvious to me that the woodlands beyond the scraped earth were an ancient forest. My memory returned to the article written by the passionate tree-hugging May Brook. She had written at length about the importance of saving the woodlands, how it was the site of ancient pagan rituals and burials, a sacred site that once lost could never be recovered.

"Seventy houses!" I whispered with a sinking in my gut. "Seventy houses on *that* land. It's criminal." Tears pricked at my eyes, my heart filling with grief. Wiping at a tear, I scolded my-self for being so emotional, and scoured the application.

It had been submitted by Elon D. Devon on behalf of Naz-tex Holdings Plc. The company name was familiar. I wracked my brain to track down that knowledge.

And then I remembered. "Selma!" I had seen the company name in her office and among all the copied emails I'd taken as evidence. One in particular, foul to the extreme in its threats, had come from an e.d.devon, the same name as in the planning application.

"So, it's not about fracking, at least not here." I paused for a moment. "The fracking story was about another site, but I bet you were onto the planning application here too." Pinning the paper back on the post, I clambered back over the gate, more confident now, and jumped to the other side.

Tyre tracks were evident through the long grass and from the uneven surface of the gouged land, the vehicle had to be a heavy truck, or more likely a 4x4 to manage the terrain. Alf had mentioned a large box on the truck, so it probably had a flatbed.

I followed the tracks to the edge of the forest where the vehicle had stopped. Here a large patch of grass was depressed and then the tracks made a wide U-turn and headed back to the gate. Whoever had driven in, had stopped here, unloaded something, then driven away. But if they had unloaded some-thing, then where was it? The cleared space was empty without even a portacabin left as a remnant of the failed fracking set up.

As I peered into the woods it was obvious just where the visitors had gone. Clumsy feet had trodden through clusters of large ferns and their unfurling leaves hung broken at the stem or squashed underfoot. Increasingly angry at this disrespect, I followed the trail.

Despite the first obvious signs of entry, the rest of their journey wasn't so clear. I walked through the woods and as the entrance became hidden, it struck me that I may not find my way out as easily as I had entered. Unlike Hansel and Gretel, I had nothing to mark my route out, but what I could use was all around me—the broken twigs and branches on the forest floor. I picked up several sticks and twigs and continued a little further into the forest, placing sticks upright along my path.

Ten minutes later, I picked up the trail of the visitors again when I came to a trodden path with fresh scuff marks in the soil. I quickened my pace and very soon my hunt was over. In a clearing stood a dilapidated cottage. Made of stone, and repaired with handmade bricks, it retained its tiled roof, but was obviously in need of repair.

Grimed windows stared blankly at me.

Scuffed earth and footprints led to the front door.

It was slightly ajar.

A bird squawked above, and the tree's canopy shivered as it took flight, catapulting from the higher branches. Startled, and already on edge, I slid beside the tree's trunk and waited. Calmer as it became obvious that the only noises in the forest were coming from hidden creatures and my breathing, I took courage and walked up to the cottage. Stale air and the scent of mildew greeted me through its open door.

Deep scuff marks were obvious on the doorstep and frame. Something big had been carried in, and it had caught the wood, gouging its damp and rotting fibres. I pushed the door open just a few inches. Inside, the room was dingey and the smell of mildew powerful. Flowered curtains greyed with dust and patchy with black mould, hung limp at the windows. An old-fashioned carpet with garish blown roses was stained with damp, greening in places and trodden with black soil.

No noise came from within the cottage. I took a step in, then walked to the centre of the room. A single armchair was placed against the fireplace, its fabric shredded and rotting. On the far side of the room were two kitchen cupboards with space for a cooker between. It was obvious that the cottage had been abandoned years ago, perhaps decades before. Items beside the chair, a pile of blankets and a cardboard box, were new.

I checked inside the box and a new chill ran down my spine. Inside were a pack of firelighters, a small can of fire accelerant, the type Pascal used when he lit a barbecue, and a newspaper—a fire starting kit! I instantly thought of the belligerent shopkeeper at the general store in the village and picked the paper out of the box. To my surprise it wasn't local. It was the same newspaper our paperboy delivered each morning for Pascal to read. Dated the day before yesterday, it carried the story of Selma Maybrook's murder with a full-page obituary on page two.

I replaced the newspaper in the box and turned to the doors that led from the living room-cum-kitchen. Both were closed to the frame but had obviously expanded in the damp atmosphere and no longer fitted. Behind the first was a small washroom that contained a narrow table. A shallow bowl and a shrivelled bar of soap sat on its top. A tin ewer, its bottom pock-marked with rust, lay on its side by the window.

The scratching noise of tiny claws on wood came from above my head. Startled, I covered my hair and stepped back into the living room, glancing at the ceiling. There was nothing to see other than watermarks where the roof had leaked. I tried to calm myself.

Heart pounding, I stood outside the second door. The thought of mice – or something worse – in the space above the ceiling, directly over my head, triggered that fight or flight response. Every instinct I had was screaming 'flight!' but I had to see what was behind that door. Something had been brought into this cottage of the damned and I had to know what it was.

I stood before the door, hands now trembling, the scurrying of hidden creatures above my head amplified in my mind.

As my fingertips touched the damp wood to push it open, I heard it!

Stomach flipping, heart palpitating, the scratching noise intense, I listened to the low moan from behind the door.

I hovered in stasis, paralysed by fear.

Chapter Twenty-Eight

Muffled moaning repeated, followed by a weak thump. The box!

Svetlana!

I pushed at the door with a tentative hand.

Grey light filtered in through grimed windows. Flowered wallpaper, tinged with brown stains, covered each wall. Mottled plaster showed where the paper was peeling and wilted. The room was bare apart from a rusting iron bedstead and an old wardrobe beside a chimney breast. The moaning was coming from inside the wardrobe.

Floorboards, dark, bare and thick with dust, creaked as I stepped into the room. A path to the wardrobe was imprinted in the dust by heavy boots.

A weak thud was followed by another moan. I took tentative steps across the floor. Wood splintered as a rotting floorboard gave way beneath my weight. I remained still then took another step forward, relieved as my foot met solid wood.

Knocking on the door I called, "Hello!" When I received no answer, I tried again. "Hello? Svetlana?"

Noise inside the wardrobe erupted into scrabbling and what sounded like urgent mewling. It *was* a woman, but her words were indecipherable.

I pulled at the door and found it locked.

The mewling became intense, the thumping louder. I couldn't tell whether she was excited or full of fear. She mewled again and followed it with a sob. Overwhelmed by the need to help her escape, I yanked at the handle. The doors yawned a little, but the lock held them tight.

"Don't worry!" I placated. "I'm going to get you out. Get to the back of the wardrobe. I'm going to kick it in."

After waiting for a moment as the woman shuffled then knocked against the back of the wardrobe, I kicked at the left door and pulled at the right. Wood splintered. I kicked again. This time the lock broke and the door flew open. Hurtling backwards as I lost my grip, I thumped against the wall.

Recovering quickly, I opened the splintered doors. Grey light revealed a cowering woman, hair awry, make-up-stained eyes full of fear. Her hands and feet were bound, her mouth gagged.

I crouched to her level. "Svetlana?"

She nodded, her eyes welling with tears.

The next moments were spent untying her hands and feet, helping her out of the wardrobe, then removing the gag. I soothed her as I worked, telling her we would go straight to the police and that she was safe with me. She sobbed as the tape ripped from her lips then flung her arms around me.

As I returned the embrace, she stiffened then pulled away, her eyes fixed to a point beyond my shoulder.

I turned to look and sighed with relief. It was Marjorie Babcock. My relief ended in the next second as another figure stepped up behind her—the towering man from the general store.

"You're trespassing," he boomed as they stepped into the room. "This is private property." Lips pursed, he seemed less than happy to find us there, and unsympathetic to the trembling woman. Standing as a barrier between them and Svetlana, I said, "This woman needs help."

"No!" Svetlana shouted. "It is them!" The pitch of her voice was hysterical. "It is Michael and his sister who kidnap me. It is them who kill Simon!"

Unable to reconcile Svetlana's statement with the Marjorie Babcock I knew, I struggled to believe that Marjorie, the uber nice, fundraising queen of the Women's Institute, was involved. It seemed impossible. "It must be a mistake, Svetlana. Marjorie's my neighbour and ..." My voice trailed off as I remembered the angry woman ransacking Selma's office, how she had knocked me flying on the stairs and clambered over me without any thought to my pain. Rage had also lain behind her eyes when I confronted her.

"Marjorie?"

"Oh, shut up Liv. You stupid fat little mouse."

"What!" Affronted by her outburst, I made an effort to express my outrage at the personal insult, but she cut me off before I got beyond a pathetic "I don't think that's very nice."

"I don't think that's very nice," she mimicked. "You are pathetic!"

"Why are you being so mean?"

"Oh, for goodness sake woman! Grow a spine. Selma bagged your husband, just like a hundred before her, but you did nothing. You pip and you squeak, fat little mouse, but do you ever take action? No. So just shut up and step aside."

I knew then that Svetlana was telling the truth and that Marjorie was intent on keeping her captive and then ending her life. Shocked by her outburst and deeply offended by the comparison to a fat little mouse, energy, dark and whirling, began to vibrate within me. Her insults were unwarranted, unkind, and more than I could take. Her lack of gratitude also stung; it had been me who had returned those awful photographs. I had been kind to the woman! I had been a fool! It was a mistake I would not repeat. At this point, I remained calm. My priority was to get Svetlana out of this death house, but I also wanted to know exactly what Marjorie was involved with.

"So," I said as my fingers began to fizz and Michael took a step forward. "It was you who kidnapped Svetlana."

"It was them!" Svetlana repeated. "Michael and old hag sister. I do not know why she call you fat little mouse, but they are the big fat rats!"

Nice one Svetlana.

Marjorie bristled at this, and Michael paused. It was obvious he was the less intelligent of the two.

"Pathetic rats!" I added, unsure of quite where this line of insult was taking me, but it bought me a little time. My anger, and the energy whirling inside my belly, felt a little more under control. "If you wanted to get rid of Svetlana, you're not doing a very good job!" I knew that the one thing Marjorie prided herself on was 'doing a good job'. At every fundraiser and event I had ever attended, she was busy making sure everything was perfect. Her home reflected this with its immaculately kept, weed-poisoned driveway and manicured privet hedge; weeds didn't even bother trying to grow there anymore. "In fact, I would go as far as to say your efforts were shoddy—a bit like your last charity extravaganza or should that be fiasco." I snorted at this in an effort to show my disdain.

The quip hit home, and Marjorie visibly bristled. "It was my most successful!"

"Sure, Marjorie. If that's what you want to believe."

"It was! Everyone said so."

"That's what everyone told you. I heard a different story. And now we have this farrago of a kidnapping. You really are losing your grip. I found Svetlana easily and now I'm taking her away."

"That is right," Svetlana added. "I go. Police will take *you*." She jabbed a finger in the kidnapper's direction but remained behind my shoulder.

"That's right, Svetlana. The police will take them and throw away the key. Don't expect a visit from me in your prison cell. You're just rubbish at this, Marjorie!"

"Hah!" Marjorie countered, eyes glittering.

Take the bait!

"I'll get rid of her if I want to, just like I got rid of Simon and Selma."

An admission! I held my nerve as I continued to goad her. "Nope. No way. I know everything and there's no way you're going to hurt a hair on Svetlana's head."

"You know everything?"

Was that a flicker of fear on her face? "Yes, I do. I know that you killed Selma, and how you did it, and I know that *he*." I pointed at the large shopkeeper, "killed Simon." I only knew that Simon had died in a car accident but given the proximity of the wreck to the village, I tried my luck. More than a flicker of concern crossed the shopkeeper's face and I felt encouraged to press on.

"And I know why you did it!" Everything suddenly slotted into place and I knew that somehow Marjorie stood to gain from the development of the land. "What you said as you came through that door was correct. This is private property. This land belongs to you." I gave each a quick glance. "You tried to get Gazcon Oil and Gas Corp. to drill here, but when the government did a U-turn on the fracking licence you decided to develop it for housing. Simon and Selma were on to you.

Marjorie made no effort to refute my deduction.

Chapter Twenty-Nine

As Marjorie stared me down without remorse or any sign that my accusations caused her discomfort, I continued. Nothing was going to stop me triumphing over Marjorie-holier-than-thou Babcock. She had severely underestimated this 'fat little mouse'! "This land is sacred, Marjorie," I said with passion, "and Selma was determined to save it, but you paid off everyone who objected." I remembered Frank Babcock's missing money. "And you raided the publishing company to do it!" Marjorie flinched at this; I was right! "Selma found you out. She was even desperate enough to stop you by taking those photographs and blackmailing you." The scowl on Marjorie's face dropped; she seemed taken aback. "And that's when you killed Selma. As for Simon, he was working with Selma to try and stop you and that's why you forced Michael to run him off the road." It was Michael's turn to look sick now. "When you discovered that it was Svetlana giving them the information, you kidnapped her too! You both killed Selma and Simon, but I'm not going to let you kill Svetlana."

A tight smile curved onto Marjorie's lips. "Well done, fat little mouse. You're not as stupid as I thought."

Riled, I decided to play with them both. "I haven't finished, Marjorie!" I threw her a huge smile. *Now to divide and conquer!* "I have some news for Michael." He looked at me with the eyes of a startled doe. "What you don't know is that Marjorie is double crossing you!" It was a lie and my brain quickly scrabbled to form a convincing story. "Her plan is to get rid of you before the sale goes through. You know she's happy to kill in cold blood and that's her plan for you. On the night Selma died, she told me about Marjorie's plans. She also told me about the evidence she had collected. I have that evidence.

"Hah! What evidence?"

"Audio recordings. She took those photos and she recorded you too." I let the statement hang there. Marjorie took the bait.

"I don't believe you. There are no audio recordings."

"Yes, there are. I know you enjoy a bit of pillow talk with your lover, Marjorie." I threw her a smile as I watched her sift through her memory.

"Her lover?" Michael scoffed. "Marjorie is a married woman. She would never have a lover."

"Of course I don't have a lover, Michael. The pathetic mouse is a liar as well as fat!"

This was going so much better than I dared hope. "I can prove it." With a solemn face I stared into Michael's eyes. "I can prove she has a lover, and then perhaps you'll believe me when I say she's a double-crossing and lying snake who wants to rob you of your inheritance!"

"Go on then!" Michael threw this out as a challenge.

A triumphant smile rose to my face as I reached into my bag and pulled out the last remaining photograph of Marjorie Babcock stark naked and in flagrante delicto with her female lover.

Marjorie spluttered.

I held the photograph aloft, holding a hand to bar Marjorie's efforts to grab it.

Michael's face blanched. "That's you! And you're with ... you're with a woman!" The shock was total.

"It's not what you think! We're in love!" Marjorie turned on me then. "I need that money! I need it to get away from Frank. If he knew about Celia, he'd kick me out and cut me off without a penny. You have no idea who he knows or what he's capable of. Oh, yes, he plays the outgoing and friendly publisher, but at home he's a grumpy, boring git with a mean streak."

"Looks like he's not the only one," I countered as she continued to scowl at me.

"The sale of this land was for me and Celia so that I could buy us a home. I've already put a deposit on a villa in Greece. We'll lose everything if we can't come up with the rest of the money before the end of the year."

Michael rounded on her. "It's true then. You want my money!"

Ignoring him she said, "We can talk about money later. No one is going to stop me getting planning permission on this land! Let's get on with sorting her out first!"

Michael seemed unsure what to do and made no effort to move.

"I can't let you do that, Marjorie," I stood to my full five-foot-four height, the heat inside me rising. "It's sacred land. If you build on it, you'll destroy it!"

"What do I care about that!" she spat.

Marjorie's complete indifference to the ancient and magical woodland, and the thought of it being destroyed, re-ignited a grief-filled ire and my inner core began to superheat. The energy accumulating was more intense than any I had experienced before. The room took on a turquoise hue then myriad iridescent particles danced before me, but a dark ring hovered around Marjorie's outline.

The woman was evil.

The limp curtains at the window twitched and, from the woodland, wailing voices rose.

A flicker of fear crossed Marjorie's face as she heard the voices and noticed the curtains.

A length of wallpaper peeled from the wall as though pulled.

Svetlana squealed behind me.

"Don't worry," I soothed as my hands fizzed. "There's nothing to fear."

With more confidence than I felt, I held my hands aloft. The burning sensation running through my arms to my fingers was intense and the energy around their tips crackled and sparked. Outside the wailing rose and I swear I heard a cacophony of voices and clashing metal. A drum seemed to beat along with my heart.

My hands sparked and as I muttered an entwining spell that came from an instinctive knowledge, the iron bedstead began to twist. It took several moments before Marjorie noticed the shaped rods of iron uncurling and breaking from their welded anchors, but by then they were snaking towards her at speed.

The voices outside rose to a cacophony as a war drum beat its rhythm. The air vibrated and the room filled with a haze of sparking, iridescent particles. Marjorie screamed and Michael roared as long lengths of black metal wound round their legs, up to their hips, chests, and heads, and locked them in an iron prison.

Svetlana took an unsteady step towards the pair, threw me a disbelieving glance as they squirmed in their cages, and grasped my arm for support. Her body trembled, and I wrapped my arm around her waist for support. "They are like fat rats ... in trap!"

Near hysterical energy burst from me as a splutter of laughter and when Svetlana joined me, we struggled to stop. Marjorie grew silent; outside the wailing voices had morphed and entwined to wail a lament.

With Marjorie and Michael unable to escape their bonds we left the house. Once in the woods, the voices rose as a chorus. Dappled sunlight danced on the bright ferns and undergrowth. "Do you hear it?" Svetlana asked as she searched for the source of the noise through the trees. I nodded. "What is it?"

"I don't know," I admitted. I had an idea of what was causing the noise, but it was fantastical.

"Do you think it is ghosts?"

I took a moment to listen. The voices sounded as though they were much deeper in the forest, but immediately around us too. I could hear chanting, a song, a drum's soft beat, and the ting and scrape of metal. All this was mingled with the shouting, then roar of men. Sensing the vibration of its energy, I replied, "I don't know about there being ghosts, but there's definitely something magical about this place."

"Da! I feel that too."

We stood for several moments, but with the quiet broken by an angry roar from inside the cottage, we ran back through the woods to the clearing and then clambered over the gate. I breathed a sigh of relief as we dropped to the other side and then made two phone calls. The first to Garrett Blackwood to inform him that the real murderers were tied up and ready for him to collect, and the second to my aunts to reassure them that I would make it back to the cottage in time for the Solstice.

Chapter Thirty

Back at the hotel, I packed my bags. The Solstice was tomorrow night, and the urge to return to Heligern Cottage was growing strong. I knew from the call to my aunts they were fretting, and I needed to be there to ease their concern. It was an instinctive draw too, as though my heart and soul needed to be there, but underlying it was the darkness of fear. I wasn't sure I wanted to go through the initiation! I'd have to leave so much behind and there was a chance that I just wouldn't be good enough. How could the 'fat little mouse' that Marjorie Babcock despised ever be as knowledgeable and respected as my beautiful Aunts Loveday, Thomasin, Euphemia, and Beatrice? Plus, there were so many other people coming for the occasion, well-respected members of their community, a community I was supposed to join. What if they met me and found me wanting—just like Marjorie had?

Whirling with contradictory emotions as I packed the final items into the suitcase my mobile rang. I instantly thought of Garrett Blackwood. Speaking to him earlier had ignited a need to see him too, and when he had said that he needed to see me and would call later, I held a secret hope that it wasn't just about the case.

I grabbed the mobile, my hands already trembling, and then sat with a thud on the bed in huge and rolling disappointment.

It was Pascal.

A pang of guilt shot through me. It was only last week that I had been on my knees with despair at his absence, and my attention was already on another man. Was I really that shallow?

I stared at the screen, listening to the ringtone, then answered.

"Hi." Emotionally and physically exhausted, I was less than enthusiastic.

"Liv?"

"Yes, it's me."

"Oh, thank goodness. I've been calling all afternoon. I was worried."

"Worried?"

"Yes! Haven't you heard the news?"

"No," I admitted. "I've been a bit busy."

"They've caught Selma's killer. She also killed Simon, her colleague at the paper."

"It's on the news already?"

"Not on the television, but that's what Dave Hepworth told me."

I was surprised at how quickly that information had travelled along the grapevine. "Did he say who did it?"

"No."

I grew a little confused. "What does that have to do with you being worried about me?"

"Well-"

The penny dropped. "You thought it was me they had in custody, didn't you!"

"Well ... No! Of course not."

Silence followed as I processed my thoughts, certain that he had suspected me though was unsure whether to feel upset or pleased that he thought I had it in me do be that proactive. I have to admit, my ego had taken a knock when Marjorie had called me a 'mouse'. Was I really that subservient? I had never seen myself that way.

"Listen, Liv ... We need to talk."

"Go ahead."

"No, not now. Later. Tonight. At our house."

Our house? "Well-"

"I'll cook and we can sit out in the garden and drink wine. It'll be like old times."

Old times? I couldn't remember the last time we did that. At one point sitting together, chatting about work, our friends, discussing our shared love for art, arguing about who was the better painter - Monet or Degas? - which the best period - Renaissance or Pre-Raphaelite? - and drinking a second glass of wine, had been the highlight of my day. We'd laugh, poke fun at one another, then fall into bed and express our mutual passion. But that had been a *long* time ago. The memory pricked at my pain. "Well, I guess we need to talk about what to do about the house. Have you contacted a solicitor?" Quite how I got those words out I'm not sure.

The line went silent, then he said, "Liv ... I miss you ... I want you back! I want a second chance, please!"

My heart thudded with such ferocity I thought it would burst. "... I ... don't know what to say."

"Please Liv. Come round and we can talk. I bought your favourite wine. A nice Chianti Reserva. I bought steak too and some of that dessert you love, from that fancy patisserie in town."

He'd remembered! "Well ..." I stalled, I knew I shouldn't, but the pain in his voice swayed me. I checked my watch. It was seven thirty pm. "I'll be there at eight. Is that alright?"

"Yes! Yes, it is."

We said goodbye and I zipped my suitcase shut with a queasy sickening in my belly. What had I just done? Given him false hope or signed myself up to another fifteen years of infidelity?

In the next moment, my phone rang again. This time the screen read 'Heligern'. I answered immediately.

Without introduction Aunt Beatrice asked, "What have you done?"

Taken aback by her unusually brusque tone, I asked, "What do you mean?"

"What have you just done?"

"Just done?"

"Yes! With that man! Pascal."

I took the phone from my ear and stared at it. Was it bugged? "Have you been listening in to my conversations?"

"I knew it! I told Loveday this morning that I had a funny feeling. And just now it came to me. You've gone back to him, haven't you!"

"No! No of course I haven't gone back to him."

"Then what *have* you done?"

"How do you even know I've done anything?"

"Oh, Livitha! Stop stalling and tell me."

I knew she would be disappointed so I said, "Well, if you know so much then you should be telling me!"

She huffed then said, "Very well. You've arranged to go back home and have dinner. He's promised you something ... something red that you like and something sweet. Hah! Yes. He's lured you with wine and chocolate. Oh, the sneaky deceiving rat!"

"Aunt Beatrice! That's my husband-"

"No, no, not him. He's nothing."

"Well, he's not nothing! I love ... loved him."

"Psht! Now listen to me ..." In the background I could hear other voices. Aunt Beatrice shushed them, complaining that she couldn't hear me if they were chattering.

"I knew it! I told you she was in danger!" Aunt Thomasin's voice grew loud. "Oh, Liv. Don't go; the Solstice is so close!"

"Ask her about the other man! Didn't she like him?"

What other man?

"I thought you said they met on the bridge. Did he give her flowers like I suggested?"

"I did my best Thomasin."

"Are you taking about James Belton?"

"No."

"You are! What did you do?" James' mesmerised face returned to my memory. He had seemed vacant, his mind preoccupied, and he had vibrated with nervous energy. "It was a spell, wasn't it! You put a spell on James Belton to make him like me."

"No, of course not, Liv."

From the background, Aunt Thomasin's called. "Tell her there are other men who will find her attractive. Maybe a soulmate. She can't trap herself again with that philandering toad."

Despite her words, all I could focus on was that my aunts had so little faith in my ability to attract a man that they had cast a spell on one to find me attractive. Had they done that to Garrett too? I felt vindicated in accepting Pascal's offer.

"Just say no to him, Livitha!" Euphemia called.

But I had already said yes, and the thought that I didn't want to become a full-blown witch, took over my thinking along with Pascal's nagging voice. 'Please, Liv' it was saying. 'Come back to me. I deserve another chance, don't I? I need you, they don't.'

"Don't you listen to him!" Beatrice hissed.

"He's not here, Aunt Bee."

"No, but he's in your head!"

Reeling that she could hear a voice that was just a memory, I shook my head to try and clear the fug.

"Why did you agree to meet him?" Thomasin called.

"He's my husband," I said in my defence, "and I swore an oath 'for richer or poorer, in sickness and in health'. Remember?"

"Of course, but he also swore to forsake all others. Remember?" Aunt Beatrice's tone was fiery.

"Yes, of course, but he's my husband and we've been married for twenty-six years-"

"During sixteen of which he cheated on you!"

"He said he's sorry and that he'll change. He just wants one more chance!"

Aunt Euphemia huffed, and Beatrice tutted.

"He's got to her!" Beatrice stated.

"We don't know that!" Aunt Loveday responded, then said, "Well, Livitha, if that's what you want ... but he must never know the truth about *us*."

She didn't have to spell it out. No outsiders were ever to know that we were witches. That knowledge in the wrong hands could put us all in danger. "Of course. I'll never tell a soul, but we're only going to talk!"

"One thing is certain, Livitha," Loveday said. "You have a choice to make."

The phone went silent and my screen flashed, 'Call Ended'.

With a creeping sense of betrayal, I drove to my own house, and Pascal. The ceremony was tomorrow night and I only had a few hours left in which to decide which path to take.

Chapter Thirty-One

The journey across town was uneventful, but as I turned into Weland Avenue a black dog ran out in front of the car. I slammed the brakes on, coming to a squealing stop only inches from the beast. The van that had followed me into the road screeched to a halt behind as my engine stalled with a jolt. The driver tooted his anger, and the dog trotted across the road and onto the opposite path oblivious to the fact that it could have been killed. I, on the other hand, trembled as adrenaline surged through my body. With my heart palpitating, I crept along the road barely moving above five miles an hour until I reached home and pulled into the drive. The van driver tooted again as he passed, and the dog watched my exit from the car then sprinted out of sight as though suddenly spooked.

Pascal's burgundy Audi gleamed in the late evening sunshine. Before my fiftieth birthday it had been a reassuring sight but now it gave me an unpleasant flipping sensation in my belly. Despite the mellowness of the evening light, I entered the house with foreboding.

The dark energy I had experienced on my last visit was still present but as I made my way through to the kitchen – I didn't knock on the front door; this was still *my* house after all – I grew a little more comfortable. Seeing Pascal at the kitchen table struggling with a corkscrew, the French doors wide open to take in the garden, I mellowed a little more; it was as though life were just slotting back together. When he turned to me it was with a flicker of joy in his eyes, as though he hadn't quite believed I would turn up. The cork released from the bottle with a loud pop and he filled a large glass then held it out in offering. "You'll love this one, Livvy – that was his pet name for me, and another relic of our past – It's a 2014 Chianti Reserva. Didn't cost much, but boy is it nice! Try it."

I had to laugh then. It was a running joke between us; somehow, he would ferret out the great tasting wine at a bargain price whilst I would grab a bargain that tasted like vinegar. I took a sip. He was right; it did taste good. "Hmm! That is nice."

On the stove a pan sizzled with our steaks and I was instructed to wait in the garden where he would serve his 'lady'. The patio table had been laid with our best cutlery and tableware. A candle, safe in a storm lantern, burned bright at the centre. The rising moon completed the scene and I waited in the late evening warmth as the sun lowered. The aroma of steak made my mouth water and the wine gave me a light-headed buzz. I felt calm and mellow, the dark energy forgotten, and, as Pascal appeared with two plates piled with salad and two perfectly cooked steaks, thoughts of returning to Heligern that night receded.

As the evening progressed, we chatted, and it really was like old times. As the meal ended and we took a walk around the garden, moonlight now shining bright and stars speckling a midnight-blue sky, he took my hand and I felt that old love return. As he talked, I listened, spellbound.

The first sign of trouble came when something swooped overhead. I dodged the missile as it flapped only inches from my head. It disappeared behind the trees, but quickly reappeared, chittering as it flew low. I was instantly reminded of my party, but made an effort to push away the memories; Pascal had talked of us starting afresh, insisting that he realised his mistake, promised to be faithful, and begged 'his beautiful Livvy' to give him another chance. He led me through the rose arch, and the leather-winged fiend only missed taffling its spiky little claws in my hair by millimetres.

As we stood in the moonlight, all thoughts of Heligern, my aunts, the bat, the Solstice, and even Garrett Blackwood disappeared. I was twenty-six again, madly in love, and being charmed into submission by my lover. His arms entwined me, and he nuzzled at my neck, his body pressing up against mine. His passion was obvious and, as he made a familiar low moan that I knew meant he was ready to take things to the next level, he whispered, "Oh, Selma," in a growling tone of desire.

I froze. He stiffened.

"I mean, Liv!"

He made an effort to pull me to him, but I resisted. I accelerated from anger to rage in ten seconds flat.

"Come on Liv, don't spoil things."

"Don't spoil things! Me!" Nothing could hold me back. The heat within me boiled over, erupting like steam from a spout. My hands sparked with a power I was incapable of controlling and words began to fill my mouth:

Tadie, tadie, yfelic tadie
I banish thee from sight, slithering, spineless wiht
Shrivel as a turd, yfelic tadie

Tadie, tadie, yfelic tadie
In a swamp shall you dwell, a green and poisonous hell
Shrivel as a turd, yfelic tadie
Tadie, tadie, yfelic tadie
Under the moon's light, under the wolf's foot
Under the eagle's wing, under the bat's shadow
Shrivel as a turd, yfelic tadie

The garden filled with white and silver streaks of light as lightning danced around Pascal. His entire body rocked with spasms and he jittered as though possessed. Then, with a final jerk, and a single throttled squeak, he disappeared.

Mesmerised by the lightning then horrified that he had disappeared, I scoured the garden for my husband. He was nowhere to be seen and I began to panic. What had I done? Somehow, I had made him disappear. A horrible vision of Pascal trapped in some alternate dimension, floating through the ether spread-eagled and unmoving as though in aspic, rose in my mind. Sweat beaded at my hairline and then a familiar voice said, "He's at your feet."

"Lucifer!" I had never been so glad to see him and scooped him into my arms. As he squirmed then immediately submitted to my embrace, I noticed the toad clambering over Pascal's abandoned jeans.

Lucifer began to purr.

I could not take my eyes off the fat and carbuncle-covered toad. Had the spell worked? Had I really turned him into a toad? "Pascal?" The creature took a hop towards me and emitted a throttled croak. I grimaced. "It is you!" With its glistening and warty green skin, and fat belly squashed and bulging against the stone, it really was the ugliest toad I had ever seen.

"Lou, do you think it's permanent?" I asked as toad-Pascal croaked, eyes bugging out and free-wheeling.

"No, I shouldn't think so," he drawled, "but then again," he said with utter indifference, "I just don't know."

Pascal gave a strangled 'grivvit' whilst overhead the bat's chitter sounded oddly like a giggle.

Chapter Thirty-Two

After folding Pascal's clothes and leaving them on the kitchen table, I placed a spare key under a pot at the back-door in case he morphed back into a man, locked the doors, and left. What I had done was terrible, but it was deeply satisfying too. I'm not a vindictive person and didn't want Pascal to remain in that form forever but he deserved the discomfort. I hoped he would also learn not to take advantage of me ever again.

It was with an angry step – how could I have even considered going back to him! – that I walked to my car. Frustration bubbled over when I saw that someone had parked across the drive. All I wanted to do now was get back to the comforting warmth of Haligern Cottage and the love of my aunts. I particularly wanted a hug from Uncle Raif.

My annoyance ebbed a little as the van's side door slid open; at least I could ask the driver to move along and let me out. The man who stepped out of the van was tall and broad and dressed in workmen's clothes. My anger died completely. He was just a working guy doing a job and parking wasn't always easy.

"Hi," I called as he stepped out of the van and began to slide the door shut. "Do you think that you could move the van? I'm just about to leave." I offered him my brightest smile, hoping that he wasn't the kind to get difficult.

"Of course." His smile was broad, and I felt reassured. "Just let me get something out of the back, then I'll be out of your way.

I scanned him as he spoke; he seemed familiar. He wasn't particularly good looking, his eyes were a little too close together, his nose just a little too thin and long, and there were several carbuncular-looking moles dotted about his face and neck, but he seemed amenable.

As he slid open the door of the van, the black dog that had run out on me earlier in the evening - the same black dog that had attacked the man on the bridge! - appeared along the road. It was staring in our direction, hackles raised, and teeth bared. It looked as though it were about to attack. It had to be a stray. Fear whirled in the pit of my belly; it could even have rabies!

Having retrieved a cloth from the van, the man stepped out, caught sight of the dog, and immediately jumped behind me. It was a less than chivalrous act, but I turned to face the dog. It barked and the man grunted. In that moment I realised why the man had seemed familiar; he *was* the walker on the bridge that the dog had harassed!

Boosted by my success at reducing Pascal to a slimy but harmless toad. I scoured my brain for something useful to use against the dog. As my hands began to fizz and a hex began to form, my world went black. I was suddenly suffocating and blind. A muffled yelp was all I could manage as a thick cloth doused in something pungent was pressed against my face.

I passed into a dark oblivion.

I have no recollection of the next hours, but my dreams were filled again with fire and grief and shadows crawling with loathsome creatures that I could only catch glimpses of.

Coming round was the most terrifying experience of my life.

Chapter Thirty-Three

Awareness came slowly. I rose from oblivion as though swimming from the bottom of a pit filled with black water. Bound to a weight, I struggled to surface, whilst beneath my feet creatures snapped, their jaws yawing, missing my toes by inches. The nightmare rode me as I kicked against the fiends in slow motion, my feet slowed by treacle-like water. Still semiconscious I broke the surface and gasped to fill my lungs. At that moment I heard a voice, its words were muffled, but soon my senses began to clear.

Blindfolded, my world was still black, but I could hear the shuffle of footsteps. The noise echoed as though we were in a chamber. An effort to move proved futile and I realised that I was bound. My shoes scratched against the floor. My ankles were tied together, and my feet barely moved when I kicked, but at least I was in a sitting position. My hands were also held down.

The shuffling grew close and then someone touched my head. I jerked and cried out through the gag filling my mouth.

"Be still, maggot!"

A man!

He continued to hover around my head then removed the blindfold. Dim light replaced the darkness and I reeled with horror at what I saw.

To my side was an old swimming pool filled with brackish-looking water. The far side wall was made up of windows, and an abandoned sun lounger was the only piece of furniture in the room apart from the table and chair at which I had been sat.

The vile odour of stagnant, bacteria-filled water filled my every breath.

I struggled again as I realised that I was tied to the chair, and my hands locked down with metal brackets to the table; the iron bracelets from my dreams! Heart pounding, I looked on with pure horror at the array of tools, browned with rust and age, laid out just beyond my hands. There was also a leather-bound notebook.

The man moved to a point where I could see him. It was the man from the bridge, the same warty man who had parked his van across my drive. I knew then that he had been stalking me, and that my abduction was pre-meditated.

The first words out of his mouth sealed his fate.

He stood on the opposite side of the table and grasped the sides, lowering himself to scowl into my eyes. "Confess thy sin, witch!"

I knew then exactly who he was; the Witchfinder General. "Matthew Hopkins!" My words were muffled and unintelligible.

"You may ask why you are here, woman. You are charged with witchcraft!" He thumped the table. It shook beneath the force, and the iron buckles scraped against my wrist. "I know thou art a witch! Confess and thy end will be less grievous."

"My end?"

"Yes, your end. All witches must die. None can live. But how painful be your death is in your power." A smirk rose to his face. "I can list the ways but burning is my favourite. You will burn regardless, but if you confess then I can drive out the imps and devious spirits before your body burns. Now ... confess!" Again, he thumped at the table, scowled then withdrew, pacing up and down as he waited for a response.

I made an effort to spark my powers and failed.

He returned to the table and fingered an implement with a spike at least three inches long. "This," he said running a finger down its spike, "is to test your devil's teat. If you be not a witch, you will feel pain."

"I haven't got a devil's teat!" I shouted through the gag as though I had no tongue.

I mentally scoured my body for any mark that could be considered a 'devil's teat'. I had a mole on my neck, but also one on my bottom. Despite the horror of the situation, I began to rile; if this foul man had undressed me whilst I was unconscious there was going to be hell to pay. I scanned my body noticing with relief that my clothes were intact, nothing unzipped or unbuttoned. Although my amulet, the engraved hammer filled with betony that my aunts had given me for protection, was missing.

"I will test your mark with this aule forthwith, but first confess thy sin! How many times has your dark lord visited to suckle at this teat?"

"A mole on my neck doesn't make me a witch!" I mumbled.

He growled, stepped behind me, and released the gag. "Now, witch. Tell me. How many times have you lain with that devil?"

"Pascal? Too many to count."

He reached for the notebook and scribbled in it. "What form does this devil take?"

"A man's. He's my husband, but my aunts were right! He's a philandering, good-for-nothing-adulterous rake!"

"Pah!" He slammed the book down. "Do not toy with me, witch!" His eyes glittered then, the whites disappearing to black. They matched the shadows dancing around his outline. I had never encountered such evil. Marjorie paled into insignificance beside Matthew Hopkins.

"You're the devil!" I whispered.

He made no effort to reply and instead reached for several metal objects on the table.

"These will help you to tell the truth. Witches are full of lies and deceit. Many have I put to death to rid the earth of their scourge. 'Thou shalt not suffer a witch to live.' It is written and so it must be."

With rapid, well-practiced movements, he attached metal contraptions to my hands. Each finger was held beneath a metal plate. Each plate held a metal bolt that would crush my fingers when turned. Sweat began to bead at my temples. My fingers felt dead and the heat at the core of my being that would usually accompany any stress was absent. Panic rose, but my power lay dormant. I made an effort to focus, my thoughts bellows blowing at dying embers. Energy sparked then died. How could my power fail me when I was in such danger?

He turned a screw above my thumb. Pain pressed down through my bone. I hissed, sucking air through my teeth.

"Confess! Tell me your sins, witch!"

"My sins?" I shouted. Adrenaline coursed through my veins, and I began to tremble. "I have no sins!"

The screw was turned again.

"Confess! Thou art a witch! Confess your sins and tell me where thy foul sisters sit in their house of lies."

Sure that he was going to torture me for the location of Heligern Cottage and my aunts, I resolved to tell him nothing, no matter what he did to me. "No! I'm not a witch. You're the evil one. You're the devil!"

"Thou art a deceiver, foul witch, and your wicked words will not hurt me." He turned a screw on another finger. "Now confess!" He quieted for a moment, then with a glitter in his eyes said, "You will burn tonight. I have the bonfire ready."

Time became unfathomable as I endured the night. There were periods of quiet where Matthew would sit and watch me. In those moments I began to nod, the oblivion of sleep a welcome relief. But as soon as my chin touched my chest, Matthew would prod me with a steel rod, and I would jolt awake. The harassment and questioning continued through the night and, as the dark took on the first hues of grey, I considered admitting that I was a witch. Let him burn me! With the words on the tip of my tongue, I heard a voice. 'Fiend' it whispered, 'may you shrivel like dung'.

The voice was joined with others until they filled my head with their song. 'Feond, feond, ferhþgeníðla. Scring þu alswa scerne awage'

I heard Aunt Thomasin say, 'In our language, Livitha. It is all the more powerful.' Her voice was joined by Aunt Beatrice's. "Say it with feeling!"

Through my pain-filled, sleep-deprived fug, I began to recite, making a subtle change to the translation that I thought
more fitting.

Fiend, fiend, mortal enemy. "Feond, feond, ferhþgeníðla."

Shrivel like a turd. "Scring þu alswa scerne awage."

"Hah!" Mathew shouted with triumph. "Thou art a foul
witch. You will not hurt me with your wicked words!"

The voices filled my head and I followed their lead, reciting
the hex. The words translated themselves on my tongue and I
spoke in the powerful language of my ancestors.

Here you will not build, nor have no home. "Her ne scealt þu
timbrien, ne nenne tun habben,

Become as nought "Naþiht geþurþe."

"Curse me, will you! Witch you will suffer before you
burn." The thumbscrews tightened.

I growled as pain wracked my fingers and hands, but I continued the incantation. *Go north, to a far town* "Ac þu scealt
north eonene to þan nihgan berhge."

Another screw was tightened and as the voices continued
to chant, my energy began to ebb. Matthew was still here, still
torturing my poor body. The hex wasn't working.

'Say it with passion, Livitha!' Aunt Loveday's stern voice
filled my mind, blotting out Matthew's cackling laugh. 'You are
a strong and powerful witch. You are one of us. Feel our power.'

The tingling, fizzing sensation of electrical currents charg-
ing in my hands began to prickle at my injured fingers, and the
dying embers of heat at my core ignited.

'Feel our power!'

Shrivel like a turd! "Scring þu alswa scerne awage!" My
voice rose with passion. Mathew's laughter stopped and he

pursed his lips. He seemed smaller. The collar of his shirt was now at his jawline, the sleeves reached halfway down his hand.

Reinvigorated, powerful energy coursed through my body. *Shrink as the coal upon the hearth!* "Clinge þu alsþa col on heorþe."

Again, Matthew's figure diminished. A flicker of fear passed over his eyes as his trousers slid from his hips. His shirt dangled over his hands.

"No! You will not defeat me!" Jumping to my side, he pulled up his shirt and twisted the thumbscrews. I screamed at the pain, but he jumped back as though electrocuted as sparks flew from my fingers.

I continued the hex. *Become as nought* "Naþiht geþurþe."

Matthew stumbled back, his trousers now to his ankles. Tripping over them, he staggered back and teetered on the edge of the filthy pool.

He regained his balance and reared at me, filling the air with expletives and threats of heinous injuries to be dealt to my body. I felt my energy wane. He may be physically smaller, but he exuded a powerful and black energy that was pushing against mine. He had centuries of practice; I only a few days. I couldn't compete!

The pain in my hands was intense and I quieted for a moment to regain some energy. He began to grow again and the dark energy, the same energy that I had picked up on in my home, began to dominate the space. He laughed.

"Stupid witch! You cannot defeat the Witchfinder General!"

As he took a step towards me, the glass on the far wall shattered and a huge black dog shot through. Landing with strength, it bounded towards Matthew and was only inches from him within seconds. Already on the edge of the pool, Mathew lost his balance and plunged into the water.

The dark and oppressive energy lessened, and I took my chance. *Shrivel like a turd!* "Scring þu alspa scerne apage!" As I shouted, my entire body sparked with energy. Bright light filled the room, whiting out the pool and the walls. All I could see was the shrinking figure of Matthew Hopkins as he flailed in the putrid water. I went in for the kill:

May you become as little as a linseed grain. "Spa litel þu gepurþe alspa linsetcorn,"

And much smaller, likewise, than a hand-worm's hipbone! "And miccli lesse alspa anes handþurmes hupeban."

And even so small may you become, that you become as nought. "And alspa litel þu gepurþe þet þu napiht gepurþe.

Shrivel like a turd "Scring þu alspa scerne apage." I shouted my power.

Become as nought "Napiht gepurþe." With those last words, all energy drained from my body, Matthew disappeared beneath the water.

With pain still wracking my hands and fingers, and the dog staring into the water, I passed out.

Chapter Thirty-Four

Bright light greeted me as I regained consciousness. I was in a hospital bed with a drip hooked up to my arm and a plaster covering the canula inserted into the back of my hand. I shuddered, panic rising from zero to ten within the second. My dislike of cannulas was phobic. All other thoughts were displaced as I became frantic.

"Get it out!" I shouted neither knowing nor caring who was in the room. "Get it out!"

"Now, now, Mrs. Carlton. Calm down. We're here to help."

"Then get it out of me!"

The nurse calmly checked the drip, decided I'd had enough of the solution, and removed the canula. It was only when she had removed the device and I had sunk back onto my pillow that I noticed Garrett Blackwood standing beside the window. I wanted the ground to swallow me up!

He grinned as I pulled the covers up to my shoulders, sidled over to the bedside, and placed a carton of grapes and a bottle of Lucozade on the table.

"Don't like needles then," he said with a wry grin.

"Have you come to arrest me?" I asked, unsure as to why he would be in the hospital. My mind was still fuzzy, and I hadn't pieced together what had happened yesterday. I remembered a dark hollow, Pascal's face, a toad that attempted to stare at me with free-wheeling eyes, and the Witchfinder General.

I sat up with a jolt and grabbed Garret's sleeve. "Has he gone?"

"Who?"

"The man at the pool. He was hurting me."

"Liv, you were found at the old park. You were unconscious, one of my colleagues brought you in. We think you were attacked. I'm going to send one of my colleagues round later to take a statement, but I wanted to check in on you."

"It was him!" I blurted, then forced my lips shut. If I started blabbing on about being tortured by Matthew Hopkins, England's notorious Witchfinder General, they'd be taking me to a very different kind of ward.

"A man. He attacked me, but I don't remember much." My fingers did remember though, they were bruised and grazed where the bolts had been screwed down.

"Just rest, Liv. You're safe now."

He took a grape and popped it into his mouth. "My mum always used to give me Lucozade when I was poorly. I thought you'd like some." He gestured to the orange bottle. It was something my aunts had done too, but only after I'd told them that's what my friend's mum had given her when she was poorly. Their usual remedy when I was unwell was a sweet brew of herbs from the garden.

"Thanks. I'll have some in a minute." I grew more uncomfortable under his gaze. I must look a state! And he was so smart in his crisp white shirt and well-cut suit.

"Listen, once this is all over, can I call you?"

Call me? "I guess so." I wanted to ask what for, just to clarify the situation, but simply nodded.

After Garrett left the hospital, I lay back on my pillow trying to piece together the last few days. His request to call me had thrown me into a tizzy too, and I was busily trying to talk myself down – it would be on a police matter, and I was stupid for believing it was anything else! – when I noticed that the sun was lowering in the sky.

The Solstice was tonight!

I threw back the bedcovers, dressed, discharged myself from hospital and took a taxi to my car.

The journey back to Heligern was frantic as I made my way through the traffic then hurtled along the country lanes. It was just as I reached the turn off for the driveway to the cottage that I realised there had been several black hairs, at least two inches long, on Garrett's pristine shirt collar. Garrett's hair was cut short. The hairs were not human.

I overshot the turning and had to back up, crunching the gears and stalling the engine twice before I managed to gather my senses. My head was reeling, but in my current overexcited state, I couldn't form coherent thoughts, and the sight of numerous cars parked all along the driveway put a halt to what I did have. The driveway was so packed with visitors' cars that I had to park in an area off the driveway between some trees. The garden was filled with members of various covens, more than usual because this year's Solstice was also my initiation.

I flew into the house, leaving my bags in the car, and entered the kitchen. I had expected some stern words from my aunts, but the energy that greeted me was riddled with doom.

"What's wrong?"

"Oh, Liv! Thank goodness you're safe. We were so worried."

"There's something wrong! What is it?" Although the aunts were busy with preparations, Aunt Loveday was missing from the kitchen. For a terrible moment I feared the worst. "Where's Uncle Raif?"

"Oh, he's out mingling with the guests. You know how he loves to chat."

Relief flooded me. "Oh, good!" The women's faces remained dour. "But something has happened?" My question received no reply. It had to be me! "I'm sorry if I've upset you. I tried to get back before now; I really did but-"

"It's not you, darling girl." Beatrice stopped my flow of words. "We have an infestation of fairies."

This surprised me. It was also one more thing that my overloaded brain struggled to process. "In infestation of ... fairies? Is that a thing?" It was possible the joke was on me; the aunts weren't averse to playing the odd trick.

They nodded with no sign of humour.

Unsure of quite why an infestation of fairies would cause such gloom, I said, "Surely an infestation of fairies can't be that bad? I thought they were supposed to be lovely sweet little creatures."

"You haven't met one, Liv. They can be horrors!" Aunt Euphemia explained.

"And they can be hell to get rid of!"

The kitchen filled with the warm glow from the setting sun as Aunt Loveday joined us. "Not still worrying about our little visitors, are you?" The aunts nodded. "Well, we will deal with them tomorrow, sisters. We have so much still to do."

"Oh, yes! It's Livitha's night tonight!"

With the energy in the room lifted, Aunt Beatrice slipped her arm around my waist. "We all have gifts for you," she said in conspiratorial tones. "You will look so beautiful!"

"Come along!" Aunt Loveday slipped her hand into mine. "Tonight, you enter your power, and everything must be perfect."

Epilogue

The Initiation

I was nervous as I stood as part of the coven circle. It was made up of at least thirty witches, and nine separate covens were represented. These were the trusted ones, our allies through the centuries, here to welcome another member to a realm barely glimpsed.

Above us the moon shone brightest silver against a velvet indigo sky pinpricked with brilliant and shimmering starlight. A fire burned at the centre of our circle, casting shadows behind our figures. I sensed the darkness beyond, the unseen and fantastical creatures that inhabited the other realms, prowling at the edge of an invisible barrier.

Hands clasped, we began to move, circling the fire.

With each step we grew faster, our song rhythmic, our voices ebbing and flowing, until all dropped to a whisper. As our speed increased, the fire burned brighter, the whispered chant more intense. Our hands were locked together, steel fingers trapping mine.

Time seemed irrelevant, my focus only on the flames and moving with the coven.

Round and round we danced in the light of the fire, our backs a barrier to the dark. Circling above us, a cloud of bats swooped and swirled in murmuration.

With each round, a single whispering voice grew loud again until there was a cacophony of chanting. Breathless, I kept pace, singing a chant that came from an ancient and instinctive knowledge.

As the voices reached a crescendo and the coven blurred with the fire, my hands were freed.

I began to rise.

Voices undulated, hysterical with joy as my feet passed their heads. I rose above the flames and hovered there, watching as enraptured witches continued to dance.

The shadows beyond the fire were dark and, like my dreams, filled with unseen creatures, their presence felt as a dark and terrible energy.

Held back by an invisible shield, they waited.

I sensed their frustration.

Hovering above the fire, I was neither of this world, or another, but as the inky sky faded, and the sun's light began to glow over the horizon's silhouette, I descended, reborn.

THE END

DEAR SISTERS,

Please join Liv and the Aunts for their next mystery!
'Hot Flashes, Sorcery, & Soulmates'[1]

---

1. https://books2read.com/u/bzjKA2

Join my reader group and you will be entitled to a copy of:
<u>'Loveday's Booke of Ancient Charmes & Spelles'</u>[2]

Other Books by the Author

If you love your mysteries with a touch of the supernatural then join ghost hunting team Peter Marshall, Meredith Blaylock, & Frankie D'Angelo:

Marshall & Blaylock Investigations
<u>When the Dead Weep</u>[3]

<u>Where Dead Men Hide</u>[4]

Printed in Great Britain
by Amazon

45623280R00135